. . . Suddenly, the speeding car was near the bridge where Jack stood. A girl, he saw, occupied the passenger seat. Then the car was out of that yellow circle of light, moving past the street lamp, becoming a dark blur. Even so, Jack kept aiming his mike at its careening movement.

There was a burst of sound.

Jack aimed the mike toward a clump of bushes.

The front tire of the car exploded.

Farther along, the car swerved and knocked down the next street lamp.

Jack was running toward the car when it crashed through the guard railing and went into the swollen waters of the creek. Once, he glanced back over his shoulder at that clump of bushes. He knew the sound, but there was no time for further thought. The car was sinking out of view, bubbles coming to the surface, mud and water surrounding it.

A George Litto Production
**A BRIAN DE PALMA FILM**


**JOHN TRAVOLTA**
and
**NANCY ALLEN**
in
**"BLOW OUT"**


also starring
**JOHN LITHGOW**
**DENNIS FRANZ**

Director of Photography
**VILMOS ZSIGMOND, A.S.C.**

Production Designer
**PAUL SYLBERT**

Edited by
**PAUL HIRSCH, A.C.E.**

Written by
**BRIAN DE PALMA**

Produced by
**GEORGE LITTO**

Directed by
**BRIAN DE PALMA**

Executive Producer
**FRED CARUSO**

Music by
**PINO DONAGGIO**


A Filmways Picture

# BLOW OUT

**Neal Williams**

*Based on the Screenplay by*
*Brian De Palma*

**BANTAM BOOKS**
TORONTO • NEW YORK • LONDON • SYDNEY

BLOW OUT
*A Bantam Book / August 1981*

ISBN 0–553–20269–3

*Published simultaneously in the United States and Canada*

---

Bantam Books are published by Bantam Books, Inc. Its trademark, consisting of the words "Bantam Books" and the por-
trayal of a bantam, is Registered in U.S. Patent and Trademark
Office and in other countries. Marca Registrada. Bantam
Books, Inc., 666 Fifth Avenue, New York, New York 10103.

---

PRINTED IN THE UNITED STATES OF AMERICA

0 9 8 7 6 5 4 3 2 1

# BLOW OUT

# 1

Sounds.

The soft evening noises: wind rustling in the trees, a faraway car horn, footsteps fading down a shadowed promenade, the indistinct words of a female voice, a door closing in some distant building.

The campus at night sent out its little murmurs. The branches of the trees undulated and sighed; in the dormitories, their windows all still lighted, the students moved in their preoccupations.

On such a night, the campus had its peculiar isolation; in the rooms of the ivy-covered buildings, the young women seemed to curl into their routines as if none of the rest of the world existed; their patterns of movement among their books, soft-drink machines, hallways, baths, and adolescent clutter became rituals; their voices rose in smug incantations; their laughter sounded like secrets; they felt private, secure, and special. Their campus, as always, was an island closed to outsiders, meant only for initiates.

Yet tonight there came a curious, deep, asthmatic breathing. A stranger moved among them.

In the shrubbery beside a ground-floor window, the stranger stopped and peered inside. There, on a bed, a soft blonde girl, dressed only in a tight T-shirt and bikini underpants, lay reading a book. She fidgeted in discontent. Her fingers moved beneath the elastic band of her panties and scratched. Her eyes darted across the pages of the book, skimming and seeing little.

The sound of the asthmatic breathing came faster now and grew more heavy. The stranger in the darkness moved closer, but at that moment two figures appeared only a few feet away, so he was forced to step back into the darkness. A boy and a girl, quietly, had appeared in the Gothic doorway not far from him. They were sneaking into the dormitory.

"Christ!" the girl suddenly said, and she pulled her boy friend into the shadowy recesses of the doorway. "Somebody's coming!"

The stranger watched all this. He saw the two huddled figures, heard the sound of approaching footsteps, and observed the door opening so that a slant of yellow light fell across the shrubbery.

As he watched, he pulled two surgical gloves on to his hands, snapping them tightly. Carefully, he kept his face in shadow.

A campus guard emerged from the doorway. He was a big man, smelling of tobacco and whiskey, and he carried an elongated flashlight. He peered into the darkness, seeing nothing, guarding nothing, then drew from the folds of his coat a half-pint bottle, sloshed its contents around, unscrewed the cap, and drank from it. The stranger and the two young people, who stood even closer, all of them hidden from view, could hear the liquor gurgling down the man's throat.

In that yellow slant of light, the stranger could see the guard's fat face and read the brass sign beyond it: Immaculate Conception College for Women.

As the guard moved away, closing the door after him and strolling off down the walkway, the boy and girl who stood in the shadows began to giggle.

"Will you shut up?" the girl said, trying to stop her own laughing.

"Sorry," the boy answered, sputtering.

"If you don't hush, we'll get caught tonight!"

Now they were fumbling with each other, laughing and breathing hard, and they emerged from the shadows of that vaulted doorway in a playful embrace. They kissed lightly, then opened the door and slipped inside. The sound of lilting disco music came from somewhere inside the dorm.

When they had gone, the stranger moved out from the bushes, kept his footfall quiet, and moved toward the music. He moved back alongside the window of the girl in the bed and toward another lighted window where two girls were dancing. They wore long, simple T-shirts that announced that they had on nothing underneath, and their movements to the disco tune were filled with thrusting suggestions. Watching them, the stranger snapped at his surgical gloves once again.

As they danced, an insistent knock came at their door, but they ignored it. Finally, swaying and grinding her hips, one of the dancers rolled her eyes and moved over to the door and opened it. It was the girl from the next room, book in hand, to issue a complaint.

"Can you turn that music down? I'm trying to study!"

"That's what we're doing," the girl at the door replied, and she kept on dancing.

"You're just making noise."

"Ever heard of modern dance? We got finals, too, and we're practicing. So get fucked."

The stranger out in the darkness stood watching and listening.

"C'mon, I mean it," the girl with the book argued.

"See ya," the dancer said with a false smile, and she slammed the door in the girl's face.

"I'm going to get the monitor!" the girl complained loudly from the other side of the door, but the dancers continued their movements.

Outside, the stranger in the surgical gloves moved on. Passing windows that revealed empty rooms, he finally reached a window, aglow in a pale half light; there, inside the room, a girl was stripping off her sweater. Pressing his face against the window for a closer look, the stranger saw that it was the girl he had seen earlier hiding from the guard. With her was the boy, who came toward her now to help her undress.

The stranger at the window listened to his own quickening asthmatic breath. It sounded deep and far away, like a groan from a cave.

They were undressing each other in a clumsy ballet of movement and embrace. The boy's pants were around his ankles, and his hands pulled down the cotton panties of the girl, who worked frantically at his shirt. Their movements were both desperate and awk-

3

wardly comical, but the stranger at the window found no humor in the scene; his mouth fell open, and his lip contorted as he pressed his face against the glass and peered in.

They were on the side of the bed now. The boy was inside her, finding his rhythm. As he continued his thrusts, though, the girl looked over his shoulder, her eyes half opened in pleasure, and saw the face at the glass.

"Oh, my god!" she cried, and tried to pull away.

By the time she had disengaged herself and had come to the window, standing there naked and gazing out, the stranger had retreated back into the shrubbery and was standing in that unmoving darkness of the moonless night.

The boy came up behind the girl and placed his arms around her.

"It was a face. Right here. I know it was," she said.

"There's nothing, see?" he said, calming her.

Together, they peered at those black leaves where the stranger hid. Yet they saw nothing, and as the seconds passed, they began to be less alarmed. The boy, in fact, began to rub the girl's breasts.

"I did see something," she said.

"You're just nervous," he told her. "Here, relax." But even as he continued to stroke her, she stood there rigid, searching the campus with her gaze. At last, the boy turned her back into the room, and the stranger, quickly and silently, moved on once again.

The dormitory was old, so its sounds were amplified: the reverberating footfall on the checkerboard tiles of the hallways, the creaking of doors and the heavy noise of their closings, the echoes of voices, and the thousands of small movements and shufflings. Its stone and timbers picked up every nuance, and in the rooms, alone, the girls could lie in their beds and listen to that old Gothic structure, picking out the familiar noises, if they wished, from those less familiar.

The stranger, inside the dorm now, looked down an empty hallway. As he began walking along it, his footsteps sent out their warning announcement. From a staircase at the end of the hall, a shadow fell across his path, though, and he stopped. More footsteps. The petulant voice of a girl, the one with the book who had been disturbed, sent the intruder behind a darkened alcove beneath the stairs.

Two girls proceeded to the door where disco music still pounded away. As they knocked and the door opened, music flooded into the hallway.

"Now turn the music down or I'm putting you on report!" a fat girl told the dancers as the girl with the book looked on with satisfaction.

"Can you believe this?" one of the dancers said to the other. "The little fink brought us the fink monitor!"

The girls were all suddenly talking at once. As they argued, the stranger slipped out of his shadowed alcove and made his way back down the hallway.

Their voices, blended in argument, threats, and insults being shouted and contorted by the echoing walls of the old building, continued for several minutes until, once more, the door slammed. For a moment longer, the monitor, a fat girl with pigtails, stood talking to the girl with the book. Eventually, they ended their conversation.

The fat girl started to go back upstairs but stopped as if she remembered something. She stood at the bottom of the stairwell, looked down the hall, then made her decision. Hurrying, as if she might be caught, she padded down to the kitchen, opened the door, switched on the light, and made her way around the chopping-block table to the refrigerator.

"I know you're in here somewhere," she said, speaking into the refrigerator. She pulled at a pigtail, looking behind a plastic bowl for some leftover cake muffins. "Come out, come out, wherever you are!" And then she found them: plump, moist, covered with icing.

As she turned from the refrigerator, the fat girl had a muffin in her mouth and one in each hand. But now her eyes flared in terror.

The gloved hands were on her throat.

She bit the muffin in half, but spittle and crumbs began to gather in the back of her mouth. The grip around her throat was so powerful and her surprise was

5

so complete that her legs seemed to melt underneath her and she swooned back in a totally yielding response. From her open mouth came a soft, gargling cough. The stranger was over her, straddling her round body, the surgical gloves locked and pressing. The muffins in her fists became wads of dough.

It was meant to be a quick struggle, but the fat monitor in pigtails, realizing that she might soon die, managed to twist her neck and upper body and to resist. She struck at her attacker, but the blows had no effect. She gagged and choked, trying to cry out.

The stranger, displeased with all the time this seemed to be taking, stumbled toward the chopping block with his victim. Their breathing was blent now: his asthmatic rasp and the girl's deep, gagging sound.

On the chopping block lay a shiny kitchen knife. Staggering with his burden, groping his way, the stranger kept his grip on the fat girl's throat as he made his way toward the knife. He nearly tripped. Then, stumbling on, he moved her ten feet across the kitchen tiles. She was beginning to pass out but saw his intention and struggled harder. Once, clearly, she imagined a possibility: he would have to release his grip on her throat in order to pick up the knife, she knew, and in that single instant she would scream. She prepared herself. Her bathrobe was open, but that was no matter. She couldn't breathe, but somehow that didn't matter, either.

At last, her moment came. The stranger slackened his grip and reached out for the knife on the chopping block. The fat girl tried to scream, but no sound came out; her throat was closed. Muffin and blood spewed out, but there was no sound. And then it was too late.

Back down the hallway, the girl with the book surrendered the idea of studying. From the dancers' room, the disco music continued to pound away, so the girl tossed her book on the bed, slipped out of her T-shirt and bikinis, and put on her terry-cloth shower robe.

The stranger emerged from the kitchen just as the girl left her room and headed for the showers but ducked back in order to watch her swaying walk as she disappeared. While he stood in the kitchen door, the boy who had sneaked in with his girl friend appeared. The stranger watched him, too. The boy tiptoed directly by, passing the kitchen where the stranger stood and making his exit through a window at the end of the hall.

The sounds of the dorm once more: each tile and timber, each door and moulding seemed to be crying out, yet no one listened.

At the far end of the hallway, in the shower room, the girl shed her robe and tested the water. Her mind was far away, not on books or dorm arguments or upcoming exams but on someone she planned to meet in a few days when the schedules and deadlines were behind her. Thinking about him, she sensed her nakedness and stepped inside the stall where a plume of steam gathered; slowly, she turned herself in the hot water, mindless of any duty or irritation and mindless, too, of the intruder who insinuated himself inside the door not twenty feet away.

The stranger's surgically gloved hands and the knife were covered with blood now, and his footfall was somehow more careless.

Inside the shower, the girl soaped herself innocently. The open stall invited the stranger, and as the girl shampooed her hair, she turned, eyes tightly shut, to face the man who had now actually moved in beside her. In that steamy cascade of water, she could have opened her eyes to see him, but she didn't. Seconds passed. The whole room seemed to call out: white tiles; her robe on its peg, the steamy clouds.

Without allowing her to open her eyes, the stranger brought the knife down hard—again and again until she began screaming.

The scream was weak and not very convincing.

"Terrible," someone said.

"What kind of a scream is that?" someone said out of the darkness.

"That's all I could get out of her," someone else replied.

"It sounds like a strangled kitty cat," another voice put in.

7

In the darkness of the mixing studio, the three men, seated behind a mixing console, watched the girl on the screen being hacked to death with a kitchen knife. It was strictly a B-movie horror film, plenty of gore and female flesh everywhere, but the scream, indeed, was a kind of plaintive mewing. Sam, the producer, stood up and started to pace. He was a paunchy, nervous, hyperactive creature in his late twenties, sweaty and worried, and he barked his orders not at his sound effects editor, Jack Luce, but at the middle-aged studio mixer who operated the equipment.

"Run it back, run it back! Let's hear that dumb scream again."

The screen before them went black. Seconds later, the image of the girl in the shower reappeared, flapping backward until the knife came out of her breast, her mouth closed, and the water continued to run back into the shower nozzle. Then the scream—playing backward on the soundtrack—came again. It was definitely weak, almost comical, and unsuitable for the required mayhem on the screen.

"Kill it," the producer said. "I can't stand to hear it again. Even backwards it sounds awful."

The mixer punched a few buttons on the console, killing the film and turning on the lights in the studio.

Jack Luce, squinting in the harsh studio lights, slumped in his chair. Like his producer and friend, he was in his late twenties, lanky, reserved, with intelligent eyes and strong good looks. He looked somehow too bright for the work he had just witnessed, but he indulged Sam, who wanted to raise a fuss, because the scream had been less than satisfactory; in fact, much of his own work lately had been indifferent.

"How long have I known you?" Sam asked him.

"Let's see. We met and went to work together on *Blood Bath,* and this is our fifth movie."

"Right, two years ago," Sam said. "You were good. I was lucky to get you as my sound man. But this is shit work."

"I admit it," Jack said. He got out of his chair and stretched.

The studio mixer, who didn't know if there was going to be a real argument or not, gathered his gear and slipped down the aisle to the exit.

"Where'd you get a scream like that?" Sam wanted to know.

"From the actress. You hired her."

"I hired her for her tits!"

"Well, maybe nobody will notice how she screams."

Suddenly, the two of them smiled.

"Look, Jack, you gotta get me some screams. And the wind in the trees. It ain't so good, either."

"I got most of these sounds out of the library. We've used most of them before."

"Okay, that's the trouble. We gotta get something new."

"New sounds cost money," Jack reminded him. "You don't want to spend money."

"True," Sam said. "But we can't make any money with screams like that on our track. You know any good screamers?"

"Girls I date tend to scream," Jack said, grinning.

"Good, ask somebody out."

"Maybe I will," Jack said. "For the sake of cinema art."


# 2


Jack Luce's editing room was also his living quarters: a giant elongated studio not far off Dock Street near the Delaware River in Philadelphia. His sound equipment took up much of the space, so the two editing benches that bore his Nagra quarter-inch tape recorder, his microphones, his 16 mm. double-system projector, his Moviola, his 16 mm. KEM, and his 16 mm. transfer machine dominated the center of his life. Against one wall his soundproof booth took up space. The opposite wall was covered with shelving—his tape library. There he had every sound any producer or director had ever needed: trains, zippers, hurricanes, explosions, flutes, rifle shots, the clink of wine glasses, and sonic booms.

The rest of the furnishings, apart from the professional clutter, consisted of a bed, its covers and sheets in disarray, and a small television set. There was a hotplate—an unused one. There was a Picasso reprint, but it was sitting on the floor turned toward the wall. All the windows had broken blinds.

It was not a studio to inspire confidence in the neatness, punctuality, and manners of its inhabitant. At this moment in Jack Luce's life, his living quarters honestly reflected his soul: tired, marginal, professionally alive, yet pitifully bored with its own mess. He was one of the finest sound editors anyplace, yet he was dubbing sound for wretched B movies in a town hardly renowned for its film industry. Once, of course, as a very young man, he had been at the top of his profession, but he had been caught in an undertow of Philadelphia politics, so that had ended. It was something he didn't even want to think about anymore. Now he didn't even do good work for Sam—they both knew it. At the bottom, one bottoms out. In recent weeks a mindless, lazy drift had taken hold of him.

He turned on his TV set and tried to work.

From his tape library he found some more wind effects, so he transferred them to 16 mm. magnetic, hoping to improve the sound of wind in the trees that Sam had complained about. Not good enough, he decided. Finally admitting that he had to get new material, he began assembling a mobile set for himself.

*Yes, yes, I'll go out tonight,* he told himself. He hoped the wind would obligingly blow. He hoped he still had the knack for finding needed material.

A television announcer was talking about Governor George McRyan, who was mounting a campaign for the presidency.

Politics.

McRyan, Jack knew, was possibly a good man, possibly the best. Yet the whole political arena vexed him. He had been burned. Once, long ago, he had been a teenage wonder with electronics and sound gear; at home, he learned to rig anything, to capture effects, to dazzle; in the army, he was the most special of their specialists; then, later, before his twenty-third birthday, he was known as a highly specialized genius in Philadelphia. His reputation brought him to the attention of the Keen Commission, an investigative body of politicians and lawmen who were uncovering corruption and alleged citizen abuses in the police department. For good pay and high praise, the young Jack Luce began to do surveillance work for the Keen Commission, helping them to expose a fabric of drug kickbacks and assorted other alleged illegal practices inside the police force. But the Keen Commission itself, he eventually learned, was tainted with political motivations—and, possibly, at times, with a desire for political vengeance. Both good guys and bad guys were on each side. A simple maze became a labyrinth; moral certainties became lost and evolved into ambiguities; purposes grew vague; what seemed clean became very dirty. In the end, because of some incidents Jack wanted to keep to himself nowadays, he retreated into his narrow work once again. He met Sam, the second-rate producer, helped to make insipid movies, and dropped out of services to such noble causes.

As Jack searched his studio for his mobile gear, the television anchorman continued talking about McRyan.

11

*year's Liberty Day celebration. Many political observers think that he'll use tonight's occasion to toss his hat in the presidential ring."*

Jack checked his battery case—ready to go.

This gear and equipment, he felt, were tangible, real, and trustworthy. One can depend on this, he told himself. But the body politic—like religion, like love, like true faith and great causes—was a kind of quicksand he intended never to walk on again. Perhaps he had been too young to comprehend all the dirt when the Keen Commission employed him, but he had seen careers ruined, even lives lost. The bruise on his innocence had become a wound.

On television, they were talking about the Liberty Day celebration. He remembered how he enjoyed all those patriotic festivities as a boy, how his mother took him around to Independence Square, to so many of the old famous houses, to see the Liberty Bell. Philadelphia seemed pristine in those days. It was before Vietnam, before Watergate, before the Keen Commission —life without smudges. He had been raised to believe and serve.

*"It has been over one hundred years since the Liberty Bell has rung, so on Liberty Day this year there will be a parade down Market Street ending at Penn's Landing for a spectacular display of fireworks. And a full-size replica of the Liberty Bell has been made of pennies donated by school children from every state in the union! Almost four hundred thousand pennies! The replica weighs over two thousand pounds—and, believe it or not, it rings! So we'll hear the sound of liberty once again after the fireworks."*

Jack switched off his TV set, picked up his gear, and went out to his car. The night was pleasantly cool. In the late spring, the sounds of summer were murmuring to life, and he wondered why he hadn't gone out more often like this. In the old days, when he was a kid experimenting with his equipment, he used to find and catalogue sounds as a matter of course. It was quiet, clever work, like catching butterflies—gentle and intelligent. He had played football, dated girls, gone to

12

dances, all that, but in this nearly secretive activity, he had always found his greatest pleasure; he was listening to the earth.

His car radio continued about Governor McRyan and the Liberty Day activities, but he soon turned it off. He drove past neighborhoods in which the walls of almost every building were adorned with murals: the giant black faces, the abstracts, and one particular one—aglow with spotlights as it presented itself on the side of an old tenement—of a pleasantly grumpy-looking bullfrog.

Driving out to Wissahickon Creek, Jack took pleasure in recognizing every neighborhood and trasition street. It was his town. And if he had entered into his first strong political cynicisms, even so he liked Philadelphia. Perhaps no man could truly represent another man. Perhaps all political activity, by its nature, was a form of corruption. Perhaps all the old values had gaping holes. Yet these neighborhoods were real, and the houses, people, murals, and life were true enough.

Driving toward his evening chores, ruminating on all this, Jack Luce had no idea that he would soon be thrust back into a world that he imagined he had abandoned.

By eight o'clock, he had driven around Wissahickon Drive, parked in a pullout alongside the cheek, and was taking his gear out of the trunk. A slight breeze was up. The park was lit by lamps, and along the walkway, not far off, a pair of lovers strolled arm in arm.

In the middle of a stone bridge spanning the creek, he held a microphone up toward some overhanging branches, hoping to get the sound of the rustling leaves. He checked his sound levels. An owl hooted somewhere off in the darkness.

He stood very still, hidden in the shadows of the overhanging branches, and for a few minutes some of his old secretive boyhood pleasures came back to him. He wasn't in nature, exactly, but part of it; sounds weren't out there in another world but within him and his equipment.

There was a snapping sound—he didn't know what it was, but his recorder took it in.

13

Down the way, the lovers got into their car—he heard the sound of the car door closing and another—somewhat nice—gust of wind that stirred the leaves.

He waited silently, and heard the soft whirr of the recorder, the water flowing in the creek below the bridge, the soft night sounds.

Along Wissahickon Drive came the sound of an approaching car. Instinctively, Jack aimed his mike in the direction of its oncoming noise.

It was a silver-gray Chrysler New Yorker, speeding recklessly, moving fast as it made a turn, its wheels squealing on the pavement. Suddenly, it was near the bridge where Jack stood, and he watched it with surprise and dismay, its intrusion noisy and complete. A girl, he saw, occupied the passenger seat. Then the car was out of that yellow circle of light, moving past the street lamp, becoming a dark blur. Even so, Jack kept aiming his mike at its careening movement.

Then there was a burst of sound.

Jack aimed the mike toward a clump of bushes across Wissahickon Drive.

The front tire of the Chrysler exploded.

Farther along, the car swerved and knocked down the next street lamp.

Jack was running toward the car when it crashed through the guard railing and went into the swollen waters of the creek. Once, he glanced back over his shoulder at that clump of bushes. He knew the sound, but there was no time for further thought. The Chrysler was sinking out of view, bubbles coming to the surface, mud and water surrounding it.

Jack dropped his equipment and stripped off his jacket as he ran.

He was not considering the danger or staying aloof or keeping cynical and detached. It had all happened to quickly. He was helping out. Later on, he would think about his sudden response: he was reverting to his old self and values, going back to form, to football and youth and the Liberty Bell, and in the excitement of the crash, he could think only that he had to act. Perhaps it had been the girl's face, illumined briefly as the car sped through that halo of lamplight so that Jack could see her wide-eyed stare.

In a single movement, Jack was down the creek bank, springing forward and diving into the muddy water where the car was already out of sight.

Meanwhile, a man ran across the road, unseen by anyone, and took note of Jack's effort. The night was suddenly quiet once more—oddly silent—and the man on the embankment could only hear his own shortened breath as he peered into the dark, swollen waters of the creek.

The car, underwater, announced itself by its glowing headlights and the eerie dome light inside the car that had been turned on by the impact. As it sank from the surface, Jack could easily follow. Swimming hard in the cold water, he reached it and saw, as if in fatal slow motion, that the car had filled with water except for a pocket of air at the rear window. There, struggling and pounding silently on the illumined glass, the hysterical girl watched as Jack swam toward her. There seemed to be nothing real in this curious underwater ballet of death: the headlights probing the muddy depths, the girl, movement, and chilling light. The girl's evening dress billowed around her. The water inside the car had grown dark with blood. Then, as the car tumbled farther down in what seemed an endless wall of muddy liquid, Jack saw the face of the tuxedoed man who floated inside the Chrysler: McRyan. Unmistakably, it was the governor, whose face Jack had seen not an hour before smiling and talking from the television set at Jack's studio. This was unreal, too, and for a moment Jack's senses reeled with misunderstanding, as if everything were a disjointed nightmare, not happening at all, a mixture of strange media imagery and actuality.

But the girl was real once more. Clinging to that tiny air space, her small fist beating on the car window, she looked for Jack as if he, too, might be part of a dream.

Jack swam to the door and tried it, but it wouldn't come open. With exaggerated gestures he signaled the girl to open it from the inside, but she seemed dazed and unable to help.

He kicked at the window, trying to break it. No use. Then, his air running out, he turned to make his way back to the surface.

Pushing upward, Jack emerged on the surface of Wissahickon Creek with a loud gasp. His thoughts flew in all directions. Swimming for shore, he told himself, *No, I can't do it, no way. The governor's already dead, and the girl can't be saved. Can't be.*

Stumbling on to the creek, he found himself on a cluster of heavy rocks, though, and decided to renew his effort. He took several deep breaths, coughing and sputtering, then picked up a large rock and returned to the dark waters of the creek. If he couldn't knock out that car window, he knew, he would have to give up. The car could easily roll on him, trapping him, and in seconds he could die with its inhabitants.

*Careful,* he told himself. *Get braced. Make the first blow count.*

When he smashed at the window with the rock, the glass gave way. For a moment, he studied his success, as if he had lots of time to ponder and consider his next move, everything returning to that same, odd, underwater slowness. Then he reached through the shattered glass and found the handle.

Nightmare time again. He was inside the car, tangled with McRyan, whose skull had been crushed and had half floated away; the man seemed to float in his softly illumined death like some exotic undersea plant. Then the girl: she was suspended in semiconsciousness, her air space gone, her dress billowing around her like blue flame. It was all clumsy and strangely graceful: water, lights, and bodies in this spectral ballet. Jack had the girl by the ankle, and they were free of the car, completely free, and moving toward the surface.

On the banks of Wissahickon Creek, Jack pulled the girl to safety. When he jerked her free from the muddy water and stretched her out, she belched out and began to cough. For minutes—endless minutes—Jack staggered around, his mind blank, until he found his jacket and dropped it over her form. Then he made his way back on to the pavement and found his equipment exactly as he had dropped it.

He was standing in the middle of the road, gathering his recording equipment, dripping wet, thoughts addled and astray, when a car came around the curve, slowed, stopped, and held him in its headlights.

# 3

The cop's little plastic nameplate said: Nelson. He seemed to be a single-minded cop who asked Jack questions there in the hospital emergency room as if Jack had been an idle bystander at the events out at Wissahickon Drive.

"You heard a bang?" Officer Nelson asked.

"Yeah, some kind of bang," Jack answered.

They occupied an open cubicle that was part of the larger emergency room. Everything was bright and smelled of coffee and antiseptic spray.

"The noise came from the left. The left side of the car," Jack explained.

"Now let's see, you were facing the car?"

"That's right," Jack said. The cop wrote all this down on a yellow pad. Somewhere beyond their cubicle orderlies wheeled patients in and out; one of those patients, Jack assumed, was the girl from the Chrysler. His thoughts were divided between concern for her and the cop's plodding questions.

"So you heard the blow out while facing the car— and you think it came from the left side? Is that right?"

"I heard a blow out, yes, but there was this bang before that. It came from the left. A bang and then a blow out."

"Probably some kind of echo," the cop reasoned.

"No, I'm a sound man. I know what echoes sound like. There was a bang, then the blow out."

17

The cop looked puzzled. "What exactly were you doin' out there?" he asked.

"Recording sound effects for a movie I'm working on."

"You recorded the blow out?"

"Yeah," Jack answered, looking over the top of the cubicle. He saw two nurses talking to each other. The girl from the car was gone.

"So what happened then?" Officer Nelson went on.

"The car went off the road, through the guard rail, and into the creek."

"And you just jumped in behind it?"

"Right. I jumped into the creek and pulled out the girl."

"What girl?" the cop asked.

"There was a girl. She was right across the room a minute ago."

The cop wrote for a long time in his yellow pad, looking mildly puzzled but attentive to duty. "You sure there was a girl in the car?"

"Sure. What do you think I was doing down there underwater?"

"Well, it must've been pretty dark under eight feet of muddy water," the cop replied, being strangely argumentative.

"You asked me for eyewitness testimony. I'm giving it to you," Jack said. "The car's lights were on—inside dome light and headlights. I could see well enough to get her out."

Officer Nelson didn't write any of this on his yellow pad. "What about the guy?" he asked instead.

"He was dead."

"You could see that? How'd you know?"

Jack stood up and peered over the edge of the partition once more. He looked across the emergency area toward a nurse coming out of a door and supposed that the girl from the wreck must be in that adjacent room.

"You saw he was dead?" the cop repeated.

"His brains were coming out of his head. I didn't exactly take his pulse, but, yeah, I figured him for dead the moment I saw him."

18

The cop snapped the pad shut. He seemed oddly angry in a way Jack couldn't understand. "What do you want out of this?" he asked Jack. "You wanta be on talk shows or something?"

"What's that supposed to mean?" Jack asked.

Abruptly, the cop got up from his chair and stalked away. Jack sat there trying to fathom what had happened. Either the cop was the governor's cousin, he decided, who suffered an undue amount of emotion over what had happened, or there was something hidden—probably political—in the interrogation.

Jack went over and peeked inside that room. Sure enough, the girl from the wreck occupied the single bed. She was propped up on those white hospital pillows, her white gown and the crisp sheets dazzling white, too, and the ceiling light illuminating all this in soft whiteness, so she looked serene and contemplative. Everything somehow made Jack want to whisper, but as he opened his mouth, about to do so, an orderly passed by in the hallway and said, "Hey, your clothes are ready."

"Thanks," Jack said, and as he watched the orderly walk on, a doctor passed by.

"You know about this patient?" Jack asked him.

"Very lucky girl," the doctor said, pausing outside the door with Jack. "Mild shock, slight hysteria, some cuts and bruises. She'll be fine."

"Can I go in? I just want to say good-by to her."

"She's been sedated, so don't stay too long," the doctor said, and he moved along toward the x-ray room.

The girl was young and attractive but not beautiful. Her forehead was bandaged, and there was an ugly dark bruise on one arm. As Jack moved into the room, she struggled to sit up in the bed. Her eyes were filled with confusion, and she seemed to be drifting toward a disoriented sleep.

"Do you have my purse?" she managed.

"No, it's probably still in the car," Jack answered softly. "I'm sure the police will get it for you."

"Yeah, but I have to leave now," she said, her voice sleepy.

19

"I don't think you can go anywhere," Jack said, smiling in spite of himself, as he stood beside the bed now. Her thin fingers were spread out on the sheet beside his hand; he felt curiously protective toward her. Somehow she was still vulnerable, still trapped, and he was responsible for her.

"You got me out," she sighed, recognizing him. Her head fell back on the pillows, and her eyelids fell and rose again in lazy acknowledgment.

"Yeah, anytime. My pleasure," Jack said.

For the tiniest second, she seemed to drop off to sleep; then she placed her hands on her face. "Oh," she said quietly, as if she had remembered something important, "I forgot. I don't have any makeup on."

"Don't worry about it. You look fine. Very pretty, in fact, now that you're not covered with mud."

"Who are you?" she asked, trying a weak smile.

"I'm Jack. Jack Luce."

"Sally."

"Pleased to meet you," he said, but this time she faded, dropping off into soft sleep before his words reached her. Gently, he placed her arm under the sheet. His feelings surprised him, just as he had been surprised to find himself in the cold waters of Wissahickon Creek. In the last few months, he had felt washed out and withdrawn; now, twice in one night, a few old, forgotten emotions—reactions, maybe, nothing more—swam around inside his blood.

"Don't leave me," she said, coming awake again.

"You need your rest," he told her. "Maybe sometime later on we can get together and have a drink."

"How about now?" she said, trying to smile once more, and he thought that she was just teasing as she struggled against going to sleep, but her leg suddenly dangled out of the sheet. She made a painful effort to rise.

"Tell you what," he said, humoring her. "I'll check with the doctor."

She pushed another leg free and came up on one elbow with drowsy desperation. He could feel the warmth from her body and smell her soapy closeness; he wanted to touch her and help her but didn't.

"They want to keep me for observation." She

sighed. "But I don't want to be observed. Please. You've got to help me out of here."

"Sally, really, there's nothing I can do."

She looked so pathetic, as if she were trying to swim out of that tangle of sheets. But complications bombarded him. If he guessed right, the noise in the hallway and emergency room outside meant that the governor's aides, reporters, detectives, and dozens of officials were arriving. That cop who had questioned him would be one of many, he figured, and he didn't particularly want to hang around for it. And if he guessed right again, Sally wanted to be far away from interrogations herself.

"I need some shoes and a coat," she explained, trying to sit up. The starchy hospital gown fell away from a smooth and nicely curved shoulder.

"You just relax," he told her, helping her to lie back on the pillows. "You hang on and I'll see what I can do."

"I've got to go," she insisted, her eyelids drooping. Beneath the sedative was a very determined girl.

"C'mon, lie down. I'll be back," he promised.

As she relented, he slipped back outside into the emergency area where the commotion mounted. Much as he suspected, the place was filled with state troopers and dozens of others.

He could see down a hallway where an ambulance crew unloaded a stretcher with a covered body at the arrival dock. The parking lot beyond was filled with police cars, lights bouncing off surrounding walls. Doctors and orderlies scurried around.

Officer Nelson escorted a man toward Jack. The man was tall, graying, and sleepy-eyed, as if he had just been dragged out of bed, but he seemed to be waking up well enough to issue orders.

"Get more men in here," he said, running a hand through his gray hair. "I want this place sealed. We don't want a circus."

Officer Nelson still seemed suspicious and oddly angry but steered the official into Jack's presence. "And this is the guy who went underwater," he told the official.

"And who are you?" Jack asked, speaking first.

21

"Lawrence Henry, the governor's friend and aide."

By this time, the ambulence crew had wheeled the stretcher into the center of the emergency area. Governor George McRyan could easily have been his country's next president, but there he was, a mound beneath some wet and muddy sheets. For an instant, the eerie images of that bloody, softly illumined car returned, but Jack forced them out of his thoughts and tried to pay attention.

"You tried to save the governor?" Henry was asking.

"He says he pulled the girl out," Officer Henry put in.

"Did you?" the aide asked.

"That's right."

"And so where is she now?"

"In that room across the way," Jack replied, indicating the door.

Lawrence Henry was clearly a man trying to think fast. His gaze fell on the door to Sally's room, then shifted from the stretcher to the cop to Jack.

"We need a place where we can talk," he said finally. "Can you find us a spare room, officer?"

"Yes, sir," the cop answered, and went off to his errand.

Lawrence Henry's shoulders sagged, and Jack knew the look. He was a man weighed down with responsibility, grief, and a public weariness. For a moment, he studied Jack as if he couldn't decide what to do with him.

Down at the end of the hallway, a half-dozen reporters tried to surge by a captain of the state troopers. One of them held a camera high and took photos of the besieged captain, who tried to smile but who clearly wanted to pistol whip each reporter.

Lawrence Henry stepped down the hallway and said, "Just close the doors and lock 'em, captain! I'll take authority in this! Nobody comes in!"

The complaints echoed up the hallway, but the captain obligingly pushed them all back toward the arrival dock. "You heard the man! Out!" he told them.

Meanwhile, Jack overheard a crew man and a

doctor as they stood talking at the emergency-room desk.

"Hell, McRyan had my vote," the crew man admitted.

"He had everybody's vote," the doctor replied, and his voice broke.

After a minute, Lawrence Henry came back up the hallway to Jack. Officer Nelson ushered them into a small examination room where Henry closed the door and leveled a straight look at Jack.

"You pulled the girl out of the car?"

"That's right," Jack answered.

"I'd like you to forget about her. I'd like you to forget you ever saw her or anyone with Governor McRyan."

A burst of incredulous, nervous laughter escaped Jack's throat. He couldn't help himself, but he tried to understand.

"What's going on here?" he managed.

"I'm the governor's friend—or was," Lawrence Henry began, but a wave of emotion overtook him, and he choked. Jack watched the man closely and knew that the display was honest, yet he was being asked to lie.

"Look, I'm sorry about McRyan," he said, "but I was there, and the girl was there."

"We know what happened," Lawrence Henry said, recovering. Authority crept back into his voice, and he was obviously a man who struggled for equilibrium. "But there's no need to embarrass the governor's family. The press is hungry. They're at the door out there. Do you have any idea what they'd do with an item like this if they knew?"

"I already told the police she was there," Jack argued.

"That's taken care of."

"Well, what about the girl?"

"I'll talk to her," the aide said evenly.

"So she'll just vanish. No mention of her in the papers?"

"That's right," Lawrence Henry said.

"I don't know," Jack said.

"It's far better that the governor died alone."

23

Jack sat down on a chrome stool beside a tilted examination table. Taped to the white wall beside his head was a needle filled and ready with adrenalin. He felt his confusion pulsing around inside himself, lots of questions roaring into his forebrain. Was the girl in danger? Was he? Was he back in the middle of political trouble as big as the Keen Commission? Would he make the right decision this time? For a moment, in the presence of the aide, he felt his youth and inexperience once again, the same as he had suffered them when he was doing dirty work for and against the police; he fell back in time and fretted that he would yield to authority and power again.

"I just don't know," he said, resisting. "I was there."

"No one gives a damn that you were there," Lawrence Henry snapped at him. "You want to tell his wife that he died with his hand up some girl's dress? You want his children to read some cheap gossip about his death in the scandal magazines?"

"No, I don't really want that," Jack said.

"Good, then cooperate. It doesn't *matter*, don't you see?"

"You're asking me to lie."

"I'm asking you not to tell the whole truth, not to volunteer it."

"And the girl?"

"We'll get both of you out of the hospital. We'll take care of it."

"I just don't know."

"Think about it," Lawrence Henry said. "I'm sure you'll figure out that it's for the best. And do me one favor, at least. Don't say anything to anybody for now. Will you do that, Jack?"

"That I'll do," Jack agreed.

When Jack crossed the emergency room again, he found Sally's room empty. Back outside the room, the area overflowed with troopers, orderlies, doctors, aides, reporters, and the normal nightly patients, the dazed and injured who watched all this commotion in the confusion of their pain. Lawrence Henry barked orders and seemed in charge. Once he turned to Jack and said, "I'll talk to the girl in just a minute. Hang on, Jack. We'll get you out of here."

For some reason, Jack didn't tell him that Sally's room was empty.

Then, as everyone hurried around, Jack spotted Sally. She stood down that hallway toward the arrival dock, her coat drawn around her tightly, her head leaning back against the polished wall. As Jack approached her, she turned her head and gave him a faint smile; her eyes seemed soft and dreamy, yet she fought off sleep and seemed determined.

"Let's get out of here," she whispered.

"The man wants to talk with you," Jack told her, taking her arm.

"The man wants to make big trouble for me," she said, sighing, and she shifted her weight to Jack's arm so that he held her up.

That deep, musty, soap-smelling warmth filled his nostrils, and he liked her clinging to him, but he also believed her: if they stayed, he somehow knew, both of them would probably get involved in a mess they couldn't handle.

He steered her toward the arrival dock where the wide doors had been unlocked to admit reporters and others. It was raining outside. Only an old janitor, leaning on his broom and sucking at a cigarette stub, watched their departure.

As Jack drove down Broad Street in the rain, Sally huddled close against his shoulder. She was wet, cold, and half asleep.

"Where do we go this time of night?" he asked.

She didn't answer.

"There's nothing open in this neighborhood. Bars are closed. How about a cup of coffee?"

"How about your place?" she asked in a soft voice, muffled against his shoulder.

"I'll bet my doorstep will be crawling with reporters," Jack said. "How about your place? I'll take you home, okay?"

Sally lifted her eyes and tried to focus on the street ahead but failed and sagged back against him. "I left my purse at the hospital," she admitted. "The reporters will find out about me, too. Let's don't go home. Let's go to a motel."

"You sure live in the fast lane," Jack told her.

"You got to help me," she whispered. "You've got to take off my clothes and get me in bed. Then you've got to let me sleep."

# 4

At the motel, things went much as Sally had asked.

She fell across the bed, asleep. Jack, in turn, took off her shoes and dress, then slipped her underneath the covers. He wiped off a raindrop that had beaded on her nose and smoothed her hair on the pillow, spreading it out so that it would dry.

Outside, the rain had stopped, and the heavy, pungent odor of coal dust hung in the night air. The sounds of the city were muted and distant: car horns, garbage cans rattling as the sanitation crews made their last rounds, a boat whistle from somewhere on the river. Jack stood beside his car for a moment, gathering his thoughts. Then he went around, unlocked his car trunk and took out his tape recorder and equipment bag.

With a headset on, he sat down in the room's only stuffed chair and listened to the playback of the accident. Sally's frail hand dangled from the covers on the bed, and she seemed, once again, vulnerable and lost and somehow his to keep, which both annoyed and pleased him.

On the tape were the sounds of that evening: the wind in the trees, the shuffling footsteps of the lovers, and the sound of them getting into the car and driving off. There was the sound of the frog and then a curious snapping sound. Jack remembered how he looked around, searching for the source of the noise. Next, the hoot of the owl could be heard—in nice reproduction.

Feeling weary himself, Jack slumped down in the old chair and listened for those next sounds: the approaching car and all that happened afterward. The motel room smelled of cigarette smoke and Lysol. Its wallpaper lined up rows of faded flowers; only Sally, her nose sticking out from the folds of the pillow, brought any beauty to the place at all.

Sleepy, he listened—a burst of sound. Then, clearly, there it was: the tire blow out.

After this, in quick order, came the sounds of the swerving car, the street lamp smashing, the metallic crash through the guard rail, and the car's crunching descent through the rocks and gravel into the creek. After hearing all this, Jack rewound the tape and played it all back.

There were two definite explosions: one was just before the blow out, another, the blow out itself. The first—he knew it in his deepest bones but just wanted to confirm it—sounded like a gunshot.

His hand went to the blinds on the window and opened a slit, which gave him a view of the wet pavement outside and the row of cars, including his own, parked before those dingy motel doorways. The gesture came from some dark little corner in him where he worried that someone might know what he suddenly knew. The street and motel parking lot, of course, were empty—no worry. Yet he caught himself in the act, giving in to a tiny wave of paranoia.

Headset still in place, he sank back in the chair once again. *Before going to sleep,* he told himself, *I'll listen one more time.* And so he did, and there it remained: two definitely separate explosions—gun and tire. He knew both sounds, naturally, from ten years of listening, but for once his knowledge didn't convert into professional use. Instead, perplexity accompanied these sounds—and a strange anxiety.

In a few hours, the morning light slanted through those blinds where he slept. Sally, sitting up in bed, regarded him with a tired smile. The earphones were still in place on his head, and his heels rested in his open shoes.

Sally got up, stripped, and took a shower. When she came out of the bathroom, she found him still deep asleep, his mouth slightly opened, and she dressed and made coffee in the little plastic caddy without waking him.

Finally, she went over and slipped the earphones off his head so that he opened his eyes.

"Hey, want some coffee?" she asked softly.

For a minute, he tried to locate himself, but her smile brought a grin to his mouth. "Good morning," he managed.

"You listening to music?" she asked, handing him his plastic cup of coffee.

"No, this is my tape recorder," he said. He sat up, rubbed his eyes, and tried to remember everything. "I do sound effects for movies."

"Sound effects? I love movies, really."

"Yeah, well, whenever you see a movie and hear a door shut or a footstep or the wind blowing, I do those sounds. I record them separately and put them on the sound tracks."

"Big movies? Ones I've seen?"

"Not exactly. This is Philadelphia, not Hollywood. We do some pretty bad stuff around here."

Sally sat on the arm of his chair. That wonderful soapy odor was on her again so that Jack wanted to touch her. She was pleasantly chatty, though, and seemed perfectly at ease, as if last night's nightmare hadn't occurred.

"Movies," she said, gazing out wide-eyed over her coffee cup. "There's an interesting subject—especially to me because I do makeup. Right now, it's only at Korvette's, but I've always had this dream about doing makeup for movies. I mean, for the big stars. Like Barbra Streisand, you know, because they don't do her right. I mean, I know how I could fix her face."

"Mm, that's great," Jack said, getting his equipment ready. "But I want you to hear something, Sally. Last night, just before the accident, I was out recording some wind sounds. In fact, several sounds. And then the car with you and McRyan came along, and I got that, too."

"You *recorded* our accident?"

"Yeah, but maybe it wasn't an accident. I think maybe your tire was shot out." By this time, Jack was standing beside her, fitting the headset on her. He had the machine turned on, and her eyes told him she was listening. "There's a gunshot sound just before the blow out. I want you to listen."

"I hear noises, okay," she responded, sipping her coffee.

"There's two explosive sounds: a gunshot, then a blow out. Hear them?"

"Well, I hear some noises," she said, taking off the earphones. "But I really can't make much out of them. I don't think I could tell a gunshot from a blow out."

"Look, can I ask you what you were doing with McRyan last night?"

"That's personal and none of your business."

"Something ugly was going on," Jack said. "You don't have to give me any details. I just wondered if—"

"I don't even know who you are," she said, interrupting him. She found her coat on a chair and slipped it on.

"Sorry I asked then," Jack said, trying another line. "Let's drop it. But maybe we should get to know each other better."

"I wouldn't mind that, but I don't want to talk about McRyan," she said.

"Let me take you home." He gathered his recording gear together while she watched. For a minute, she didn't say anything; then he noticed that she had a slight smile for him.

"I live with a girl friend, Judy Demming," she said. "But, sure, you can take me home if you want to."

"I want to," he assured her, throwing the strap over his shoulder and flashing a grin. She followed him out to his car and stood in the sunlight beside him while he loaded things into his trunk.

At the motel office, Jack stopped to pay the bill and bought a morning newspaper. McRyan's face dominated the front page. When Jack returned to Sally in the car, he placed the paper on the seat between them, so she had to look at it.

"I still don't want to talk about him," she told him.

They drove toward the address she gave him without saying much. The streets, he felt, were particularly dreary: pools of gray water left from last night's rain, blocks of row houses, smokestacks and discolored bricks. He let the silence build between himself and Sally.

"I guess I felt I could ask you anything," he said at last, "because I pulled you out of the car. I guess I felt that made us friends."

"You got me out of the hospital last night, too," she reminded him.

"Right, I did."

"We'll talk," she said finally. "Maybe later on."

The promise was good enough.

That afternoon, he sat in his editing studio transferring the quarter-inch tape of the accident onto 16 mm. magnetic tape. He played everything over: the wind in the trees, the lovers, the frog, the odd snapping sound. At that one, he stopped the recording several times, reversed, and played it again, wondering what exactly he was listening to. It had some resemblance to a wire being raked across a rough surface, but that wasn't it exactly.

Getting out a reel, he took the 16 mm. transfer and rewound it for permanent storage on the reel. Then, once more, he threaded it through a sound reader—slowly. At half speed, he listened to the same sounds: gunshot, blow out, the lamp smashing, the guard rail breaking, and finally the splash in the water.

He was absolutely sure.

He labeled the reel, then tried to go to work on that horror picture Sam wanted him to finish, but he thought of Sally and her soapy warmth, McRyan underwater, the telltale sounds on that reel nearby.

As he worked at the Moviola that afternoon, and the daylight hours faded into dusk, he thought about his hated work with the Keen Commission.

It had all started because of complaints against the police for abuse and brutalities. An investigative group took a special look at police tactics regarding blacks and found a number of abusive cases, but things began to go deeper. There seemed to be cops on the take. There seemed to be an in-group of cops who, despite rank or assignment, appeared to have power over other cops.

Jack had a couple of good black friends at the time who told him about various incidents, and when he was first contacted to work for a new commission, he was sympathetic to its purpose. He went by the office on Market Street to meet the man who would become his immediate superior, Tom Bell.

"We can't have a police force which is a law unto itself," Bell explained to him. "The force has to account for itself and can't be a closed system."

The idea sounded right to Jack, who asked how he could help.

"Some of the work we want you to do might be dangerous," the commission officer told him. "But we want to break what some of us consider a closed system. We want the police to be the public servants again, not public masters."

They were sitting beside a window that overlooked the river. Everything out there Jack loved: the neighborhoods, the smog, the playgrounds, the Eagles, the Phillies, the river, all of it. He had been adopted by every city street. Since he had been a kid, he had known where to get the best pasta, the best basketball court, the best girls, the best free music, anything. Now his city pride and his vision of himself coincided; he was young and ready to take risks; he was a good technician and a good citizen.

"You want to help?" Tom Bell asked him.

"Yeah, sure." Jack replied.

"Good, we'll work out a pay scale."

"I want two fifty a week," Jack said, being a good Philadelphian.

"Hey, that's steep."

"I checked. The commission has federal money. It can afford to pay its technicians."

"I like you, Jack. You're a smart boy," Tom Bell

31

said with a smile that wasn't exactly warm. "And you better be. Some of it will be tough."

All this was almost ten years ago, and it was tough and changed Jack's mind about himself and everything else.

# 5

At first, he bugged some apartments and bars, trying to document payoffs to cops. It was sleazy work, and only a short time passed before he felt like an evil little mole who burrowed into holes from which there was no retreat.

One cop was in love with a prostitute named Darva. He moved her out of her ghetto brothel, found them an apartment, and treated her like an adored wife, but Darva clearly meant to take vengeance on the cop for a reason Jack never understood. On his day shifts, she opened herself for business, like a store with regular hours. She turned six to ten tricks daily, so traffic and conversation in the apartment was always heavy, and Jack, sitting there in the basement listening, became fascinated with the inevitable drama. Darva was so flagrant that it became clear that she meant to be caught.

The cop phoned home during the day. Sometimes Darva talked with him on the phone—also bugged— while some client relieved himself between her legs.

"You sound funny," the cop remarked during one such session. "You okay?"

"Doin' real good," Darva told him, and when they finished their conversation and she had hung up the phone, Jack could hear the echo of her laughter from the other bugs in the apartment.

The cop was on the take, but his money was all spent on Darva and his new home life. He bought new bathroom fixtures, a color TV set, and built shelves in the foyer, yet for all his domesticity he never seemed to notice the mud tracked in by strangers, the cigarette stubs in the ashtrays, or other signs of Darva's daytime sexual marathons.

"Your job is finished when you get that cop to say how much he's taking or who he's getting it from or what he's doing to earn it," Tom Bell told Jack.

"He won't say outright."

"Stay with him."

"And the situation is running me crazy," Jack complained. "He's gonna find out about this bitch and shoot her. I'm going to record a bloodbath."

"Don't worry about what happens with the romance," Tom Bell told him. "Just get something on tape about the cop and his money. We want only that."

From his chair in the basement, sitting and waiting, Jack felt like one of Darva's clients: a participant in the deception, a contributor to the consequences that were bound to come. He ate Ritz crackers and drank Pepsi and listened. At times, of course, he left the recorder going and took long walks, but then he would have to listen to the tapes again to make sure he hadn't missed anything. The pay was all right, but he needed a partner. And the work became obsessive, keeping his body and mind fixed in the sordid melodrama upstairs.

Was this public service? Was this what his skills amounted to? He knew Darva's breathing in the sexual act as well as he knew his own.

Finally, inevitably, the cop came home at midday to find the truth, but there were twists and ironies in store.

"Hammy! What are you doin' to me?" came the cop's voice on the recorder. "I can't believe it's you!"

"Me and twenty others, you geek," the male's voice replied.

They shouted at each other while the visitor got dressed. Darva punctuated their argument with an occasional profanity.

All the visitors to the apartment had been other cops, colleagues and pals. It was some sort of punish-

33

ment, as best as Jack could figure, in which the cop upstairs was clearly the helpless outsider, taking this humiliation at the hands of his own kind in a kind of elaborate retribution. The cop began to cry and wail as he understood this. Darva was packing. And it was all bound up with who was on the take, who wasn't, things that had happened that were now vague history, none of which, finally, could be comprehended from those pained and bitter words on the tapes.

Cops against cops and citizens against citizens—the ambiguities of the Keen Commission, for Jack, were just beginning to reveal themselves.

After Hammy and Darva had vacated the apartment the last night, the cop went into the bathroom, closed the door, put his head down on the newly bought lavatory, and cried and cried. His sobs were magnified by the bug on the drainpipe, amplified, and turned into a torrent of pain as they were recorded on the tapes down in the basement.

Jack was young in those days and tough but hardly tough enough for that. The next day, he went on to his next assignment.

The next cop was Timmy DiPrima, who wore flashy clothes, drove a Porsche, ate at gourmet spots, and generally attracted so much attention that everyone on the investigative teams assumed he was heavy on the take. Jack bugged his apartment, too, but got mostly reels and reels of silence. DiPrima was a quiet sort at home, never had any guests, and made phone calls only to his mother and sister, both of whom he seemed to be supporting and caring for like a devoted son and brother. Occasionally, he played a Mozart record. He didn't own a television set. After a week, Jack told all this to Tom Bell at the office.

"The kid's loaded," Tom Bell argued. "He's making connections somewhere. Keep the bug on him another week."

The same thing: a week of such absolute quiet that Jack, across the street sitting at the recording equipment, took long naps that messed up his sleeping habits.

Toward the end of the second week, Jack listened while DiPrima told his sister on the phone that he had to go out but would leave the apartment door unlocked so that she could come borrow an electric wok from his kitchen. Knowing he shouldn't think of it, Jack calculated that he could peek inside the apartment during the interval between the time that DiPrima left and the sister arrived. When the Porsche pulled away from the curb across the street, Jack left his station and strolled over. As announced, DiPrima's door was unlocked.

The cop had a large three-bedroom layout on the second floor, but it was without furniture except for a bed, record player, refrigerator, phone, and a single kitchen chair with a broken leg. The bugs, Jack knew, had been installed in heating vents, so the agents who did that work had never actually been inside DiPrima's rooms. So the surprise was complete: DiPrima was a gardener. The rooms consisted of rows of shallow boxes filled with dirt and nourishing some of the largest and most beautiful marijuana plants Jack had ever seen.

The kid wasn't on the take.

He was a man of private enterprise.

For a few minutes, Jack stood there breathing the stuff and almost got high with the green beauty of it all. He liked to hit on the stuff himself. He admired the scale of the operation, the neatness, the bravado.

For another day, Jack went back to his recording equipment and tried to think about the fate of Patrolman Timmy DiPrima. Actually, he reasoned, the young cop, who was breaking the law, wasn't breaking the particular law being investigated by the Keen Commission. He wasn't involved in a shakedown. He wasn't using police muscle to exploit helpless citizens. He was just producing high-quality grass, working his best every day, and taking care of his widowed mother and a sister who was going to college and trying to learn how to cook Chinese.

"What have you got?" Tom Bell asked him at their next briefing.

"Nothing. I think DiPrima's clean."

"How can he be clean? He's a goddamned playboy! Look at his suits and his car and all his tabs when he's off duty!" Bell was no more than thirty years old himself: one of those coiffed and sharp-talking law-school types who wanted to score in legal services, run for attorney general, run for governor, and get to the big political trough with all the others. Jack didn't like Bell, didn't like his own job, and, at the moment, listening in on the life of Timmy DiPrima, didn't much like himself.

"Well, I think he's clean," Jack persisted. "He's got family money, you know."

"Who says?"

"His mother's a widow. I think she got a big insurance settlement, and I feel certain DiPrima got something from his dad, too."

"You think so?" Bell asked, weakening.

"Yeah, I heard a lot listening to phone conversations. That's how it is."

"Okay, wrap him up. We got bigger fish," Bell said, making a decision.

That evening, Jack knocked on DiPrima's door when he knew the young cop was home. "You can't come in," DiPrima shouted through the door. "Whatcha want?"

"I came to talk about your pot plants," Jack called, "and if you don't open up, I'll go get the building superintendent, who has a master key."

DiPrima invoked the name of the Blessed Virgin and opened the door a crack. "Who are you? What the hell are you talkin' about?" he asked.

"I'm a guy who has been bugging your apartment. You've been under investigation by some people I can't tell you about. But nobody knows about your indoor crop except me."

"What crop?" DiPrima asked, bluffing.

"You got big street value in there with you," Jack said. "Let me in. We don't want to discuss this in the hallway."

Jack was admitted and told DiPrima the whole story—except that he didn't divulge the nature of the Keen investigation and warned the young cop about saying anything to anybody.

"Internal affairs committee," DiPrima said. "That's it, right? I'm being investigated by internal affairs?"

"Not exactly," Jack said.

"And how do I know you're not lying?"

"In that heating vent, you'll find a bug," Jack suggested. "It's not working now because I've disconnected all my equipment. But my people took the trouble to rig a bug from inside your walls. If they'd walked into this place, they'd have found all your box plants. But they didn't, so you're cool for now."

"What do you want?"

"Give me a bag for my personal use," Jack said, smiling.

"That's it?"

"Yeah, that's all. And take care of yourself."

DiPrima gave him a pound and suggested that he could always get more, but Jack went away and never bothered him again. He got busy with his next assignment, so he never knew if Patrolman Timmy DiPrima moved, kept on growing his garden, or became scared and quit. He envisioned big things for that apartment house: floor after dirt floor of six-foot plants and DiPrima as a king of pot, but time and circumstance prevailed against his ever knowing.

Weeks passed, and sometimes he didn't even work. There was a short assignment bugging a place in Chinatown, but great trouble arose: the commission failed to find a Chinese translator who could make out what was being said on the reels.

While his work continued, the Philadelphia cops managed to stay in hot water with civil-rights lawyers, community groups, and plain citizens. Firearms were used in simple traffic arrests, a suspect was half beaten to death before he was discovered to be an innocent man who in no way resembled the wanted robber, and residents of a tenement attacked a cop who got carried away beating a fourteen-year-old black kid. The police chief and mayor stood by their men in blue. They blocked charges against cops accused of excesses, intimidated those who filed complaints, and denied all charges of corruption.

Jack didn't like the chief or mayor, so he favored, in general, the Keen investigation, yet he suspected that politics were being played and suspected, further, that good cops who were doing their duty and risking their lives for low pay were getting unnecessarily hassled.

"You're right, it's all dirty," Tom Bell said during another of their briefings. "But some of it is a lot dirtier than the rest—and you're not hired to make a distinction."

"I'm planning to quit," Jack said.

"Good, let me know. Meanwhile, I got another job for you. Can you fix a wire on a man?"

"Wire somebody for sound? I think I can."

"We have this informer. We want him to meet with some cops, get them talking, and confirm what we think we have on them."

"I can put a wire on him they can't even feel if they frisk him," Jack said.

The informer's name was Freddie Corso, a cop who for years had busted drug dealers, then had taken their drugs back on the street—to sell them himself as a dealer. He was that mixture of immorality and sentiment Jack had seen on the streets all his life: a guy who would kill, rob, deal in drugs, and betray his friends but who would also give to the poor, who sponsored a neighborhood youth club, and who could suddenly show extreme loyalty and dedication, in his own capricious way, toward family, strangers, or those same colleagues he had previously disowned. Freddie laughed and sweated continuously, mopping his face with a handkerchief like an Italian trumpet player—which, in fact, he also was. He was the epitome of the happy street cop; he knew everybody and managed, each day, to either please or infuriate those who knew him.

"The guy never knows himself what he'll do next," Tom Bell explained about Freddie Corso. "Every day in his neighborhood he's either gonna rip somebody off or help somebody or both. He'll risk his life to save some black kid; then next day he'll sell the same kid his first hit of drugs. He'll take some looney rapist and reason with him and get him to a psychiatrist; then he'll slug some motorist with a weighted sap just for back talk. Whatever else, he runs his precinct. He's one visible cop. My own theory of Freddie is that he's hyperactive. He's Robin Hood and the devil because he can't sit still."

"But he was definitely caught dealing?"

"Yeah, he got the choice of either going to jail or informing. In this particular case, he decided to get morality."

Freddie Corso came to Jack's house—Jack was still living at home with his mother at the time—and while they watched the 76ers play the Knicks on television, Jack fitted him with the wire. Freddie was as expansive as ever, cheering the 76ers, sipping beer, sweating, and offering Jack extra money.

"You're a nice kid. Here," he said, peeling off two twenties. "Just a little extra for this." He stuck the money in Jack's shirt pocket.

Mrs. Luce, Jack's mother, wandered into the living room at that moment with a bowl of popcorn. Jack complained that he didn't need Freddie's money.

"Look, buy your sweet mama a present," Freddie urged. "Treat her right. She don't get many favors livin' with you. I'll bet you tinker around with your sound equipment and the girls on the block and you never take care of your mama."

"You've got that correct," Mrs. Luce replied. She obviously liked this loud, generous cop who stood there with his shirt off, his undershirt pulled up, and a wire around his waist.

"Hey, look at that!" Freddie said, eating a mouthful of popcorn and pointing at the TV set. "You see what Doctor J did with that ball?"

The next night was not so much fun. For Freddie Corso's first assignment with the Keen Commission, he had set up a meeting between a corrupt police captain and one of the East Coast's known mob figures, a Mafia lieutenant who was a specialist in dealing drugs to black school children. Tom Bell and the whole commission force were on the case that evening, ready to follow the trio in their car and ready to listen to their conversation over Jack's wire. Jack had strapped a tiny microphone and transmitter—so small that they could be tucked under the belt—around Freddie's waist—and blocks away, in a car or aparment, anywhere, the commission members could pick up any sound within ten feet of their informer.

It was a long, terrible night; Jack remembered it well.

They met at the Napoli Restaurant where the mob lieutenant was finishing supper. After greeting each other—every voice was wonderfully distinct—they hopped in the mobster's car and drove out Germantown Avenue, while Bell, Jack, and two armed commission members followed in an unmarked Chevrolet.

Freddie complained that he didn't feel good.

The mobster and the police captain, meanwhile, began to argue.

"I seen you havin' espresso with your brother-in-law last week," the captain said to the mobster. "I'm gonna have to report you to the parole officer for that."

"What the hell are you talkin' about? This was supposed to be a friendly meeting. You gonna give me shit?"

"You broke your parole. You been fraternizing with a known criminal again. You can get your parole revoked."

"We was gonna talk business tonight," the mobster complained. "This is cheap shit. Freddie, you said this was gonna be cool."

"I'd be willing to forget what I saw for five thousand," the captain said boldly. "Then we can get down to business."

"You want five grand to forget you saw me with my brother-in-law?"

"Right. Then we can deal drugs and favors."

"You're a scumbag," the mobster said. "Christ, I gotta pay a bonus to begin talkin' with this scumbag, Freddie?"

"I don't feel so good," Freddie repeated.

"You're sweatin' again, Freddie," the police captain said. "Maybe you got a fever or something."

"We set up this meeting to talk straight. I got to pay some scumbag money before we even begin," the mobster complained.

In the following car, the commission members

40

were joyful. Every word was beautifully incriminating. In his excitement, Tom Bell pounded Jack on the shoulder and squealed with laughter.

"First things first," the police captain affirmed. "You gotta take care of your parole before you can deal with me. I don't want no loose threads."

"I'll offer a thousand," the mobster said. "Not a penny more."

"Well, that's a start," the captain said.

"Pull over at that service station," Freddie whined. "I think I'm sick."

"You didn't eat no pasta tonight," the mobster told him, pulling off the street. "You grabbin' your stomach like you ate too much."

"Yeah, it's my belly. I'm goin' in here and use the can," Freddie said.

In the following car, Jack noticed that the static from the wire around Freddie's waist had increased. He worried that something might be going wrong with the wire, but the sound of Freddie's footsteps into the gas station, the opening and closing of doors, even Freddie's labored breathing told him that the equipment was still working.

"Oh, my God, oh, me," Freddie said. He was in the bathroom at the gas station. Later, they learned that Freddie was sweating so profusely that the battery attached to the transmitter under his belt was shorting out and burning a hole in him. His nerves had caused a malfunction, and he was in a stall inside the gas station, tearing his clothes open, trying to disconnect the wire, when the mobster barged in and found him.

"Sonavabitch," the mobster said. "I thought so."

It was the last sound or voice they heard from the wire.

For several minutes, the commission members sat in their car in the dark shadows across from the service station until the police captain and the mobster came out alone, got back into their car, and drove away. Then they went across the street and found Freddie.

He was hanging by Jack's wire from the toilet stall, his neck broken, his eyes bulging.

Jack quit working for the commission the next day.

As the years passed and he recalled his work for the Keen investigation, he understood that his sense of right and wrong altered forever. If he had used morality as a motivation—and in some small corner of himself he had done so—he would never do it again. Freddie Corso was no saint, but his grotesque death worked a profound impression on young Jack Luce. He would stay clear of causes, he promised himself; he would avoid committment. Never again.

This was why, now, years later, the evidence on his reels of sound tape disturbed his deepest nerve ends. McRyan, he felt sure, was assassinated. Yet some monstrous irony had revealed this to him alone, he felt, so that he had to juggle the knowledge inside his own complicated consciousness.

He didn't want the responsibility of knowledge.

Of course, he didn't fully and absolutely *know*. Doubt remained. If he wanted to keep things to himself, he knew, he could always rationalize doing so. He didn't have to go to the authorities with his educated guess; no one else was a sound technician, and no one else could even substantiate his evidence. It was as though he had been handed a scroll written in a special language, with a hideous prophecy that had been made clear to him alone.

Sitting in his editing studio, he absently worked at that horror movie. The stranger on campus moved through the shadowed recesses of the night—sound of the wind in the trees, sound of footfall.

His thoughts went astray.

No, he didn't know absolutely—at least not so that he could explain with any certainty to anyone else. And who would he tell? The police? Not likely. There might even be the possibility—he hated to think so—that they knew about the gunshot, that they knew it was murder, and that they were part of some wild conspiracy that would ultimately make the Keen Commission seem like a moral simplicity. No, he would finally tell only himself; truth was a hideous prophecy, he supposed, that one read in secret and kept in secret. It came to each man in his own language. It was deciphered in the heart. And its curse, he felt, was perhaps that it carried with it the necessity of silence.

# 6

Early that evening, Jack was still at his editing bench when Sam, his eyes wide, his paunch bouncing, came through the door and without speaking ran over to the TV set and switched it on.

"Hello, Sam. Come in. Turn on my set. You missing Walt Disney or something?" Jack asked, grinning. He had never seen his producer in more of a hurry.

"They got movies of McRyan getting killed!" Sam told him. "I heard it on the car radio! I think they've got it on the news tonight!"

Sam switched channels until, finally, he found the proper one. There was a shot of McRyan's silver-gray car being hauled out of the creek on Wissahickon Drive. The TV anchorman was droning on.

"Films of the crash? Can't be," Jack said. He put down a reel of tape and switched off his equipment.

"Quiet, listen," Sam told him.

The TV anchorman stared out earnestly from the set, saying,

> "Incredible as it seems, then, a local photographer, Manny Karp, was on the scene of the accident last night with his camera. 'Eye on the City News' has learned that late today Mr. Karp sold his film to News Today magazine for an undisclosed sum of money. Our own Frank Donahue spoke with Mr. Karp just a few minutes ago outside the magazine's offices."

"Unbelievable, isn't it?" Sam asked, pulling a candy bar out of his pocket and unwrapping it as he watched.

"You don't know how unbelievable," Jack answered.

43

By this time, Manny Karp, surrounded by reporters and the newspaper interviewer, Donahue, a bright-looking young man in sharply tailored clothes, stood talking to each other before the cameras. Karp talked out of the side of his mouth and blinked heavily between words.

"So I went out there to try out some new film stock, right?" Manny said to Donahue and the other reporters, trying to sound credible but somehow not quite making it. "Very high-speed film, see, for night shooting. I do lots of work at night."

"Sam, this can't be true," Jack said.

"But it is. Listen."

"All of a sudden, I hear this car screamin' down the road. I hear it start skidding. I wasn't even really thinkin' when I turned around. I kept my camera runnin' and watched it go through the rail into the creek."

"Was Governor McRyan in control of the car?" Donahue asked.

"In control? No way he had control. He went right into the water."

"And he was alone?" Donahue asked.

"I didn't see nobody," Karp replied.

"So why didn't you go to the police last night? Why didn't you show the film to them?" Donahue asked.

"I wasn't sure I had the shot," Karp explained, smiling a little. "Today I realized what I had, so I gave it to the people who pay. The cops got their copy, sure, but if I'd gone to them first, I wouldn't got nothin'."

Sam's mouth was filled with candy as he said, "Lucky devil. Imagine gettin' photos of a big event like that. I'll bet he made a bundle. Incredible."

"Yeah," Jack said. "It is." He stifled the impulse to tell Sam what he knew himself. At the same time, a hundred questions came to him. Where was the photographer while he was standing on that little bridge with his sound equipment? Wasn't it all too coincidental? Did the photographer fire the shot? Was there a massive conspiracy—far beyond his wildest imaginings?

That evening, Jack and Sam went back to work

44

on the sound track for the horror film, but Jack's thoughts were far away. The gore on the screen, Sam's chocolate mess, the soundless TV set glowing across the room, the reels of mag tape, all filtered through Jack's consciousness in dim and distant ways. When they finished late that night, Jack wanted only to get by himself so he could think things out.

"Don't you want a sandwich and a beer?" Sam asked him.

"Not tonight, thanks."

"One more session and I figure we're through with this movie," Sam said, standing at the door.

"I'll see you tomorrow, maybe," Jack replied, dismissing his boss.

He watched Sam trudge downstairs and heard the door shut at the bottom of the landing. Then, his thoughts still tumbling, Jack went inside and leaned against the wall, staring at the silent, glowing television set and hearing Manny Karp's rasping voice. He decided that he would try to get those photos. Possibly, he could synchronize photos and sound so that the evidence would be irrefutable. He already knew he was right about the gunshot, but somewhere in his deepest fears he felt that he might need to prove his knowledge to others. The best course, naturally, would be to let things alone—seek nothing, find nothing, know nothing. But that way was already decided against.

The next day he went to South Street. In a cheap, run-down neighborhood of secondhand bridal shops, pawn stores, seedy bars, and paint-peeled warehouses, he found Manny Karp's sign on a second-story window: KARP PHOTOS: BABY PORTRAITS, PASSPORTS, WEDDINGS. The stairway leading up to the studio smelled of urine and crushed-out cigarettes.

A city cop, a young guy whose smile was nearly a sneer, guarded Karp's door. With his chair tilted back against the wall, the cop leafed through a stack of shiny 8 by 10 photographs. Jack approached slowly.

"Can I go in?"

"He ain't there," the cop said. "Whatcha need?"

"I've got to pick up some pictures," Jack lied.

"You anybody?"

"Just a customer."

The cop's mouth made its sneer, which seemed less like a smile than ever. He turned over another photograph in his stack and rubbed his eyes as if they were already weary of seeing Jack standing there.

"You're a reporter," the cop said. "You want to get a piece of Kark's film of McRyan. Everybody who comes upstairs wants the same thing."

"No, really, I'm a regular customer," Jack went on. "He told me to come by. There's supposed to be a packet on his desk."

"Know what I got here?" the cop asked. "Dirty pictures. Whole stack of 'em. And that's all that's inside there, too. The guy really does divorces. This particular photo I got on my lap shows some old geezer pulling the blankets up to hide his face. He's in a motel bed. The girl has nice tits. And from the look on her face I think she expected the photographer, but the old guy didn't."

He turned the photo around so that Jack could see it.

"If you're a customer, you might be a lawyer, but you ain't dressed like one. You might be a husband, but I don't think so. I figure you're a reporter like everybody else I've seen today."

"Karp does all kinds of photos," Jack went on, still bluffing. "And I need to get my pictures. Know where I can find him?"

"Mr. Karp is very popular. But he ain't in town no more," the young cop said, delivering his smiling sneer. He turned to another photograph, and Jack couldn't help looking: the old man, the girl with her legs boldly opened, the harsh glare of the flashbulb.

"You know where Karp has gone, then?" Jack continued.

"No, buddy, I don't. But I got a feeling he ain't comin' back soon—maybe never. That office in there don't look too neat. Somebody took the electric fan, and the phones are disconnected."

"Well, thanks, anyway."

"Always glad to be of service." The cop sneered as Jack walked away.

Outside the smelly stairway, Jack stood on the

street and tried to gather his thoughts. With the cop, he had concealed a recognition.

For a moment, he felt that he was back underwater, swimming in a muddy flow, images dimmed and confused, duties and tasks impossible, faces blurred, causes lost, doors tightly shut.

The naked girl in the photo had been Sally.

# 7

At a magazine kiosk on Chestnut Street, the banner displayed over the counter announced EXCLUSIVE PHOTOS OF MCRYAN'S DEATH. Jack stood there paying for several copies of *News Today* magazine and talking to the bald proprietor, who shook his head sadly and repeated, "A tragedy, a tragedy."

"I suppose he had your vote," Jack remarked, having heard the same from everyone so far.

"Best politician in the city since Ben Franklin," the old man snapped.

Jack turned pages until he came to the photos. They were in sequence, as he had hoped. For a minute he stood beside the kiosk, its magazines, papers, and lottery tickets flapping in the soft breeze, and studied Karp's work.

He drove toward the film offices with a sense of both foolishness and determination. Why am I doing this? And if I get conclusive evidence, he asked himself, what if I turn out to be serving some darker side of politics? Like all technicians caught in such questions, he already knew the answer: he would chase things out to the end. The result of nuclear investigation is atomic explosion, he knew, and the warrior ultimately develops his skills so he can fight. In the same way, the sounds recorded that night made sense and gave proof—important proof—of something. He had to know.

The film offices were housed above an old cinema just off Locust Street. A closet-sized reception room led into Sam's office; then a corridor opened into a series of storage and editing areas. A stairway led into the old movie house where Sam screened his work.

Debby, the receptionist, was a high school girl with oversized breasts who had gone to work for Sam for minimum wages and with the expectation that she would soon be a film star. She sat at her desk reading another Harlequin romance.

"Is Rick using his office?" Jack asked as he came in.

"No, he's out, but Sam wants to see you right away."

"Tell him I'll talk to him later," Jack answered, and by this time he was in the corridor, his magazines underneath his arm, heading for the animation room where Rick Talley, a rangy dopehead who edited most of Sam's material, had his office in one corner. Jack locked the door behind him.

Cutting the blowups out of the news magazine, Jack carefully mounted each one on heavy white paper, numbering them in sequence. The quality wasn't good but would have to do, he told himself, and he worked steadily until he had eighty shots in all—every frame of Karp's film from before the blow out to the crash off the bridge.

At the animation stand, then, he set up the lights, checked out the camera, and loaded it. Carefully, one at a time, he photographed the magazine frames.

One series of five or six shots especially won his attention. He noticed that Sally didn't appear opposite the driver's seat.

As he was nearly finished, a knock came at the door.

"Jack, you in there?" Sam called. "Come down to my office, will ya, Jack?"

"Sam, I'm busy on some stuff. See you in a few minutes," he called.

"I got somethin' good," Sam said. "Hurry up."

The work was slow and boring, but Jack didn't

mind it. The room held him and guarded him for a moment, and he liked its silence. From two posters on opposite walls, Greta Garbo and Clara Bow smiled at each other.

When the job was done, Jack took the film out of the camera and stacked up his mounted blowups.

As he passed Sam's office on his way out, Sam yelled at him. "Get in here! I got somethin' for you!"

"I can't talk now. I have to run," Jack countered, still trying to leave.

"I want you to meet Sherry Roman," Sam said, opening the door wider so that a tall, buxom brunette was revealed sitting on his desk.

"Pleased to meet you," Jack offered.

"Get in here," Sam said, grinning. He ushered Jack inside and closed the door. Sherry Roman made coy moves with her shoulders.

"Okay, honey, show him what you can do," the producer said.

Obligingly, Sherry slipped out of her suit jacket and in one swift move yanked her T-shirt over her head. When she shook out her hair, her enormous breasts bounced from side to side. A moment of profound silence followed.

"Yeah, so?" Jack asked.

"She's gonna scream," Sam explained, smiling with what seemed the pride of artistic discovery. "She's gonna try out for the horror movie. You still need a screamer, don't you?"

"Yeah, but why'd she take off her shirt?" Jack inquired.

"Why *not?*" Sam asked, as if such questions absolutely missed the point. Then he turned to Sherry, who had a tendency to glance over one shoulder, turn, then glance over the other. "Go ahead, honey," he urged her. "Scream."

Sherry Roman filled her ample lungs with air and screamed. Afterward, Jack could hear Debby, the receptionist, jumping around her desk outside the door and loudly asking what was the matter.

"Whatcha think?" Sam asked earnestly.

"Keep looking," Jack said evenly. He made his exit.

"Damn, I knew I wouldn't be good enough," Sherry Roman pouted.

"Don't worry. We'll find you something else to do," Sam told her, and Jack was gone.

His next stop was a film processing plant. Norris, an old high school friend, ran the business for two lawyers who had foreclosed on the previous owners and had taken over. It was in good hands because Norris, now as always, was energetic, organized, and a kind of genius, Jack felt, who had never found his thing. In the old days, they made model airplanes and cars together, so Norris always smelled like glue. He had also introduced Jack to archery, baseball cards, and, finally, sound effects. They used to record sounds, using everything from tin cans to old upright pianos, on Norris's little portable recorder.

"Old buddy," Norris said in greeting, as usual, and they slapped each other's shoulders in the old salute.

"Got some amateur stuff here," Jack told him. "I shot some pictures out of *News Today*—not very good quality. I want you to create a filmstrip for me so I can run them through my Moviola. Can you do that? And can you improve the quality of each shot? And can you do it cheap?"

"You seen Linda Spain lately?" Norris wanted to know.

"Not lately. Why?"

"I been thinking about her. She was a girl friend of yours—let's see, how long ago? Three years?"

"Longer. I think she got married."

"I'll do you this favor. You do me one. If you ever see Linda Spain again, tell her I want to prove I love her. Tell her that. She'll understand. Will you do it?"

They both laughed.

"I didn't know you liked her."

"You always got the girls," Norris said. "Jack Luce got every girl in sight, and you know what I got? Hobbies, like archery and chess. Remember?"

Their laughter echoed around the walls of Norris's glassed-in office at the front of the plant. When they were too weak from laughing, they sat down in chairs across from one another.

"This is real important to me," Jack said, holding up the roll of film.

"I can do a filmstrip, but it will take time," Norris said. "I can also improve the quality of each shot because one of my big hobbies nowadays is photo lab. And I can give you a good price: free. But you owe me a good word with Linda, old buddy, because I've been dreaming about her at night."

"A man should have his dreams," Jack philosophized, and they laughed again.

When Norris took the film out of the office, Jack picked up the phone on the desk and dialed Judy Demming's number. Sally, sounding rushed, answered, and Jack said hello.

"Jack, I just can't see you right now," she told him. "I'm on my way to Reading Station. I'm going to visit a friend."

"Maybe I could meet you there," Jack suggested.

"My train leaves in an hour, so I don't have much time," she replied.

"Look, I'll meet you there. We'll have a quick drink, then you can be on your way. Okay?"

"Well, all right."

She sounded less than enthusiastic, so he drove over to Reading Station with the mild suspicion that she might not show or might put off talking to him until another time. But there she stood at the information booth where they had agreed to meet. She had her luggage with her and looked beautiful in a gray suit and conservative high-heeled shoes, so much like a pretty teacher or librarian, in fact, that Jack forgot having seen her, undressed, in those dreary photos outside Karp's office.

"I only have twenty minutes before my train," she said. Her smile seemed genuine and right.

"Come on," he told her, taking her arm. "Just one drink."

He moved her in the direction of the depot bar, an old-fashioned place beyond the newsstands with racks of wine glasses, mahogany, and worn tiles. He

51

stacked her luggage beside them as he slipped into a booth with her. Instead of sitting across from her, he deliberately crowded in beside her, smiling and talking as their thighs touched. She was laughing as he told her how much he liked waking up in the morning with strange girls across the motel room while he slept in his earphones.

Their drinks came, and he ordered another round.

For a half hour, he kept her busy, talking more than he usually talked, touching her arm, moving his face close to hers so that, at times, he caught the pale scent of the perfume that rose from beneath her clothes. She sipped her drink and fixed her eyes in his. By the time she had finished a second, she had missed her train.

"I've missed it!" she said, not seeming too distraught.

"Good, I'm glad."

"Oh, my, listen—what was I saying? I know it was something important."

"About the models and their makeup," he prompted her.

"Right, the models. When you see them without makeup, they look totally different. Only with makeup do they look like glamour girls."

"I've noticed that."

"Makeup is a philosophy of life," she confided, slurring her words a little and smiling. "I mean, what's the first thing you see when you meet somebody?"

"Their face," Jack answered, guessing correctly.

"Exactly. So the face has to look right or nobody ever gives you a second look. The face is the mirror of—" Sally paused, trying to remember the quotation. "The face is the mirror of the—"

Jack switched glasses so that she would finish his drink.

"Every face needs makeup," she concluded.

"No, not yours," he said, taking her hand.

"But a face shouldn't *look* like makeup. I've hidden my face. You don't see makeup, but you don't see my face, either. In fact, it may not be there."

"I can't believe you're wearing makeup," he went on.

"I am *only* makeup," she confessed. "But I don't have the makeup look."

"No, you look natural."

"It took me two hours this morning to fix a face. Makeup is my life. I don't know if I have a face anymore except I know——" She paused, trying to gather her words and thoughts. "The face is the mirror of the soul," she said, getting the quotation at last.

"That's probably true," he said.

"You're not interested in makeup," she said, smiling a tipsy smile. "I think maybe you just kept me talking so I'd miss my train."

"Well, true, I don't want you to go."

"Why not?"

"Because we just met. And we need to get to know each other."

"You're nice," she said.

"Let's go to my studio," he said. "Let's go there and take off all our makeup."

His face was close to hers; for a moment, it seemed they might kiss, but they didn't. "Oh," she said, still slurring her words a little, "that's the nicest thing anybody's said to me in a long time."

He put her luggage into his car, drove to the studio, and for a moment they stood inside his doorway viewing the clutter of his life: all that equipment and those overflowing tape libraries. Then he turned on the little blue light above his editing bench.

"This looks——I don't know——important," she remarked, and she strolled across the room, untying her belt as she went. The sound of a boat horn came from the river. At the window, she turned; in that soft illumination of distant neon, she took off her clothes as she talked.

"You don't know me, and I don't know you," she said. She was slightly drunk, but it seemed just an excuse to let the poetry come out of her. "But I've gone on a long trip, all the way to California and back, and every mile of the way I was mutilated. It was like that trip took my face off. I wasn't me when I got out there——and I've been just a makeup job ever since I got back. Which was years ago, in fact. I've been just cosmetics and memory, and now I can't even remember who I was. I can't recall why I wanted to go to California."

She was so stunning naked that she took his breath away. Unlike those tawdry photos, she had a serene sexuality about her tonight in that neon softness; she had her hands in her hair, stroking her hair, as if she tried to massage away whatever burned her brain, her breasts pulled high, one hip jutting out.

"It was such a long trip and, funny, now I can't even remember why I meant to catch that train tonight. Oh, my, the trips I've taken. I can't even remember them all, so I'm glad I'm here."

Only when he put his mouth on hers did she stop talking. Once again, as before in the hospital, she seemed soft and vulnerable, and that perfumed, soapy musk came off her body announcing that it was her own true scent. Her breasts flattened out against him, and he forgot why he had brought her here; he forgot that he wanted information from her, that he was using her in any way, because somehow, now, she seemed to be using him.

His bed was a pile of old mattresses and pillows banked up in one corner of the studio. There, for hours, she moved as if she were never drunk or the least out of control, and at last he fell asleep with her, their arms and legs entwined, her deep, soapy warmth filling his dreams.

Then, in the morning, she woke up talking again.

"I'm not always going to work at Korvettes," she began. "I'm not a salesgirl at the cosmetic counter, not down inside myself. I think I'm an actress."

While she talked him awake, he got up and made coffee on his hotplate. The room seemed warm from her glow; over on those sheet-tossed mattresses, she sprawled out in an unashamed nakedness, and he couldn't take his eyes off her.

"But you have to tell me about yourself," she said finally.

"There's not much to tell," he said, moving beside her again.

"Tell me how you became a sound man."

In spite of himself, he began to talk, too. He told her about living with his mother, putting together his first equipment with Norris, going into the army where he worked as a sound engineer over in Jersey, coming back and working for the Keen Commission.

"You were a cop?" she asked.

As he poured them their first cup of coffee, he told her the stories about Darva and her cop husband, Tony DiPrima, and his apartment full of pot and Freddie Corso and the wire that burned him up. He became graphic about Freddie Corso, and Sally placed her fingers over his lips.

"I quit working for the police after that. I got into the movie business—if it can be called that."

"It wasn't your fault," she said about Freddie.

"Tell that to him."

"It wasn't. When life goes wrong, you can't blame yourself. He volunteered to do what he did."

She strolled over to the hotplate to refill their cups, and he watched her gentle undulations. Now or never, he told himself, and he devised a way of talking to her about McRyan.

"I assume Lawrence Henry talked with you, too," he said, gambling.

"Yeah," she answered absently. "He talk with you?"

"Sure," he lied.

"That's why I was leaving town," she admitted. "He gave me enough money to disappear for a couple of months. I guess you figured that."

"Sally, they're covering up a lot more than the fact that you were with McRyan that night. I'm sure the tire was shot out."

She brought his coffee back to him and silently began to put on her clothes. He was afraid to say anything else for a minute.

"How can you be so sure?" she asked.

"Did you see those pictures in *News Today*?"

"Yeah, I saw 'em." She reached behind her back and fastened her bra. She meant to leave, obviously, as quickly as she could. He knew that he had only a little time to convince her.

"I figured out a way to put my sound with those magazine pictures," he told her.

"Really?" she replied, stalling as she dressed.

55

"Yeah, and when you see the photos and sound together you're going to see it wasn't a blow out."

She stopped a zipper and just stared at him.

"Look, Sally, don't leave town just yet. Stick around a couple of days and help me. Will you do that for me?"

"Jack, I'm in enough trouble already. If I stay here—"

"Please," he said, getting up and putting on his old robe. He came over to her and took her face in his hands. "Once I understand all this—and get clear of it—we can disappear together."

"You mean it?"

"Sure. We can go anyplace we want."

"Florida, maybe?" She put her face against his chest.

"Anyplace you say," he told her, and he didn't know if he meant it or not.

# 8

Sally found herself back at her apartment staring at her luggage, thinking of how she would explain her return to her roommate and wondering how she allowed Jack Luce to talk her into staying.

"Another guy," she said, sighing in the empty room, and she felt that she should be on the train heading south, as she had meant to be.

The luggage at her feet reminded her of her trip west when she was just out of her teen years; it seemed like a forlorn symbol now, scruffed and used, like Sally herself. That trip was her life: mutable and changing, filled with painful compromise. Yet she couldn't really run away, not with the help of payoff money, not with anyone's help, and not with her own past dragging behind her like so much ballast.

She thought of Jack, who was handsome and tender, and she wanted very much to run away with him, as he said, but she knew better; at the end of a long run lay another sticky life, another place to run from, another man to escape.

She felt like a whore and a wanderer. Putting her clothes back into the drawers from which she had taken them only a few hours before, she had a mild satisfaction that Jack wanted her help—and seemed to want her. But staying itself seemed like a trap, too, as if in some corner of herself she was running toward hope one more time. In spite of herself, she felt gullible and foolish.

That trip years ago: she had forty dollars and the same luggage when she started hitchhiking on the turnpike heading west.

The man who picked her up called himself Stew, and he drove a new Mustang and seemed to have plenty of money.

"How far you going?" he asked her.

"All the way west. I don't want to stop until I see the Pacific Ocean."

"Then that's how far I'm going," he told her. His smile should have told her something, too, but didn't.

After a few miles, he talked about nothing but sex, and his language and overtures became overt and harsh. Even so, she made up her mind that the price of the trip could be paid because she was no virgin and no prude. The high school basketball player had made her up against the brick wall at the rear of the gym. She had put out in cars, in movie houses, in city parks, in the pews of the Catholic church near Washington Square. She had walked out of that tenement house filled with drunken, broken lives—her mother's and father's included—and had given herself freely to a world that demanded commodities and services. Not all of it was pleasant by any means, but time had toughened her, she felt, and the prospect of a quick ride to the Coast was worth anything.

She was wrong.

"We're going to stop early tonight, and I'm gonna wear you out," Stew told her, and she tried to smile.

He was tirelessly brutal. "Here, get down, goddammit, get down here," he yelled at her, and he began beating her even before their first embrace. While she serviced him, he grabbed a fistful of her hair, pulling and pushing her backward and forward, and with his other fist he squeezed her fingers until she thought they might break. Afterward, she spat and cursed him and—although she tried not to—broke into tears. It pleased him immensely, but he slapped her so hard that her lip bled and covered her body with a slick gore as he took her.

"Oh, stop, stop it," she implored him, but he had an enormous energy that seemed to feed on her pain.

Later, when she tried to lock him out of the bathroom, he kicked the door open. She wanted to escape, but he forced her to lie down beside him in bed, throwing his leg across her, and in spite of herself she fell asleep. The next day, they drove out of the motel at dawn.

"Stew, you don't have to be so mean," she told him that second day. It had occurred to her to try a new tactic: she would submit and be sweet.

"You excite me, honey. I couldn't help myself," he told her.

"Well, you're too rough. Be nice and I'll be nice."

By noon, when they stopped for lunch, they had told each other all their lies. She had won a scholarship, she told him, and was going to a famous drama school on the Coast. His father was rich, he explained, and he intended to drive around the country until he "got his head on straight." He meant to go to Oregon, he said, and maybe Canada. In spite of this exchange, she assumed he was dealing drugs and that he probably knew her for what she was, too.

That night, beyond St. Louis, things were worse.

When she resisted, he beat her senseless. When she was unconscious, he violated all the orifices of her body, and when she staggered into the motel bathroom crying and moaning, he came in saying, "Shut up. I don't want to hear no more blubbering."

"Can't help it," she sobbed.

"Yes, you can," he told her, and he choked her into silence. For a while, bent back over the toilet, his hands on her throat, she knew she would die. White and red explosions ignited before her eyes, and only when she passed out again did he let go. Afterward, she lay on the cold linoleum of the bathroom floor, deciding that she had better stay there while he slept in the bed; she curled herself into a naked ball, but pain signaled from all over her body and kept her awake. Toward morning, she crept onto the rug at the foot of his bed.

She had to escape but decided to ride with him another day, covering as much distance as possible. After all, they were heading due west, flying along. She would find a policeman or even a sympathetic motel clerk when they stopped. She wouldn't go into a motel room with him again.

But Stew seemed to know her limits in all things. That evening, they pulled into the Red Barn Steakhouse outside Amarillo, Texas, and somehow he knew that she would be terribly hungry. Once again, she decided to stay with him just through the meal, so they went inside and ordered thick filets and beer. For a few minutes, he seemed relaxed and cordial, as if he had brought her out for a dinner date, and when the food arrived, she ate greedily.

"Nice, isn't it?" he asked her, with his thin little smile.

"Real good," she said. "I appreciate it."

The Red Barn's jukebox played overloud country and western songs and its decor of branding irons, horse tack, and cowboy paintings gave it an atmosphere conducive to loud talk, dancing, and whooping. Pitchers of beer floated by in the hands of buxom waitresses. Young studs in jeans, boots, T-shirts, and Stetsons stomped around the dance floor. For a few minutes after her steak dinner, Sally enjoyed the ruckus and forgot that she had to get away.

Then a plump, loud cowgirl came over and insisted on Stew dancing with her. Sally didn't know what would happen. She thought Stew might hit the woman. But, finally, curiously, he consented, and the two of them stomped out onto the floor to the rhythms of "Cotton-Eyed Joe."

For a minute, Sally watched them dancing, then got up, waving to Stew as she left the table, and went to the women's room.

There, she saw herself in the harsh glare of the mirror. Her eye was black, and her neck was bruised. She had a vision of his bending her over a toilet again, murdering her, and she determined to get away as quickly as possible.

The lounge was set off from the dining room and dance floor, so she made her way, unseen, to the parking lot.

There she stood, miles from home, desperate, in some godawful place called Amarillo, in a graveled lot filled with pickup trucks and Cadillacs. Two cowboys with toothpicks stuck in their mouths were climbing into their customized pickup down at the far end of the lot beneath a street lamp. She hurried toward them.

"Can I get a ride into town?" she called.

They stopped and turned toward her, each man standing with a truck door open, one boot propped up inside the cab.

"We ain't goin' to town, but you can sure come with us," the one nearest said. He had a kind face, like the Marlboro rancher.

"Then let's get going," she said, coming into the light where they could see her face and the discolored eye.

"What happened to you, sugar?" the Marlboro man asked. "Boy friend beat you up?"

"He sure did," Sally answered. "And he'll whip all three of us if he comes out and finds me. Let's go."

The two men exchanged confident smiles.

"Ain't nobody gonna hurt nobody," the lanky kid on the other side of the truck promised.

"Like we said, we ain't goin' toward town," the older one went on. "You sure you want to come with us?"

Sally nodded yes.

"We also might be headin' toward some fun. You up to some fun tonight?"

"Please," she said, worried.

60

"Oh, oh, here we go," the lanky kid said with a little laugh.

Stew's Mustang pulled up in a shower of gravel and dust. As he got out and came toward them, Sally saw that he grinned with a strange, oddly charming expectation. "Howdy," he called, like one of the good old boys.

The men at the pickup truck had tight smiles.

For a moment, all of them paused and waited as the tension gathered.

Then Stew grabbed Sally's arm and hurled her toward his car. "Get in there," he snarled at her.

The Marlboro man grinned, seemed as if he meant to say something, and took one small step forward, but without warning Stew whirled on him and in a fluid, deadly kick brought a foot cleanly into the man's crotch. The cowboy grunted and bent forward. As he did so, Stew kicked him again, bringing a knee to his chin and driving him against the side of the pickup.

The lanky kid was on his way. Before he got there, though, Stew had the older man sprawled and helpless. "Hold on," Stew told the kid as he came around the side of the truck. "If you come on, I'm gonna kick you silly. Then I'm gonna gouge out one of your eyes—I swear to God I will." The threat was so specific and filled with such a hiss that the kid stopped in his tracks.

The man on the ground, leaning against the side of the pickup, groaned.

"Get in the damn car," Stew told Sally.

Then, because the man's legs lay open, Stew kicked him again. It was a vicious blow to the groin, yet the kid only watched, his mouth hanging open, as his friend took it.

"Goddamit, you believe what I say, don't you?" Stew asked the kid.

The lanky kid said nothing, watching his friend helplessly.

Stew kicked the man again.

Sally wanted to urge the kid to help out, yet she said nothing because the fight was clearly over—except for Stew's meanness.

"What's the matter, don't want your eye gouged out?" Stew hissed, and he delivered a final hard kick to the fallen man's groin.

The man tried to say something, perhaps the kid's name.

Then Stew brushed by the kid, who stepped aside, and opened the door of the Mustang, throwing Sally inside.

They drove in silence for a while. When they were beyond the city limits of Amarillo, Stew ordered her to find something in the glove compartment.

"Taped to the top of the compartment," he told her. "A tin box. Pull the tape loose."

He took two of the pills and ordered her to do the same, so she did. Not long afterward, drowsiness overtook her, and she fell asleep, her head propped against the vibrating window. When she woke up, they were parked in a roadside stop, the pastel mountains of New Mexico all around them, and she felt all her pains, as if he had beaten her again during the night.

They drove all day again—at speeds above seventy—and took pills every couple of hours: reds and speckled ones. He seemed oddly content, as if the fight and the pills had brought him to some new frequency where he listened to his own hard music. Again, Sally became hopeful that the night would pass in peace.

That night was the worst.

When she was gone on the pills he forced her down, he beat and violated her. She knew she was badly hurt and prayed that someone in that little clapboard motel on the edge of nowhere would come knock on the door to interrupt his anger, but no one came. Once, he took towels, wrapped them around her, and hit her through their soft cushion so that he wouldn't break her skin. Even so, she was a bloody mess when he finished.

"Stew," she whined after he hit her and she had fallen around his ankles, grabbing and holding on.

"That's not my name, you stupid bitch," he told her.

*He's going to kill me now,* she thought.

"That's not my car outside, either," he went on.

"You never saw me before. You ain't here. You're lost."

The next morning, he drove her down the highway, casting occasional glances in her direction as she slumped across from him. "You look awful," he growled at her, and, in truth, she looked so beaten that he knew he couldn't be seen with her. At the side of the road in the middle of the desert, he stopped and pushed her out. He tossed her luggage in the middle of the lane where he had stopped. No cars were in sight for miles in either direction.

"C'mon, don't," she begged, as if she really wanted to go on with him. She wondered if some corner of her brain had been knocked loose, yet she pleaded with him. "Don't leave me out here. Take me with you."

He drove off, and she watched the Mustang disappear over one hill, then another, until the horizon swallowed it up.

An hour later, a state trooper drove up. She sat on her luggage on the shoulder of the road, her head in her hands. She learned later that the main highway was miles off. "My God," the trooper said when she raised her face to him.

After that, she sat in an unlocked jail cell in some little town on the wrong side of a mountain waiting for a doctor who never arrived and listening to rock music on a plastic radio above some law officer's desk. The lawman's uniform was indistinct, as if he belonged to some foreign army.

"Where's that trooper?" she asked the officer.

"He's gone, girlie, and ain't comin' back," the man said.

She sat listening to the music, trying to think.

"What state is this, anyway?" she asked.

"You don't know?" the officer asked, laughing big. He went into a back room and never answered her question.

Late that afternoon, she began to worry and complain. When she suggested making a phone call, the lawman locked her in the cell.

"I didn't do nothing," she said, weeping. "I'm hurt!"

"You sit quiet," he warned her. "You're a vagrant, girlie. Up until now I been nice to you."

Thoughts and worries came to her: her luggage, internal injuries, being a prisoner in this tiny cell for months, dying alone and unnoticed.

That night, the lawman came into the cell, locked it behind him, and slowly took off his clothes. He placed the key on a nail above her bunk. He was a large, hairy man, perhaps fifty years old, with the odor of cigarettes about him; his chest sagged as if he never exercised, yet his arms hung thick and heavy like cables. The only light slanted across the floor from that back room, and she watched his movements while he undressed as if she dreamed them in a stupor.

"Be nice to me now," he told her, "and you'll get out of here in the morning."

"You promise?" she asked.

"I do promise," he said. "Now you be nice."

He came down over her like a heavy, reeking tent. As he took her, she could look over his shoulder at that key dangling from the nail.

The next morning, he brought her a plate of soggy pancakes from the back room and told her that he had arranged a ride for her. "Pal of mine goin' to Phoenix," he said. "You treat him right and he'll be real good to you. He's got himself a big air-conditioned Lincoln."

The salesman's name was Eddie Whitt, and he drove the back roads.

"What do you sell?" she asked, making conversation.

"I'll sell you if you don't do right," he said, laughing aloud.

"That's not funny."

"Hell, it ain't meant to be. I can drive across the border not a hundred miles from here and set you down in a Mexican cat house. You'll be doin' tricks for tortillas five years from now and glad to be alive."

After this threat, they drove fifty miles in silence.

"I need to get to L.A.," she said at last.

"What for?"

"I got business. I need to get there in a hurry. Is

there anything I can do for you so you'll drive me all the way?"

"I don't know," Eddie Whitt said. "I'll think about it."

Another fifteen miles went by.

"Don't beat on me and I'll do anything," she said. "My eye's black, and I think I've got a loose tooth and internal injuries."

In another minute, Eddie Whitt pulled to the side of the road and began to unfasten his trousers. There were no towns on this barren stretch, virtually no traffic, and Sally couldn't think of any defense. Her body was too broken and her spirit was too weak, so she could only ask, "You want me over on top of you, Eddie?"

"Hell, no," he said, and she knew well enough what that meant.

He slipped off his shoes and pushed off his trousers while she counted the pain and soreness in her body. Roughly, he pulled her down toward her job, but, even so, he was gentle compared to Stew.

He finished quickly and lay back, his head on the seat rest, his eyes closed; for a while, she thought and hoped he might be dead.

"You okay?" she asked him. The interior of the Lincoln was littered with crumpled Kleenex.

"You sit still and behave yourself," he ordered her. "I got to take a leak." As stern as he sounded, Stew had been so much worse that she wasn't afraid anymore—only deeply determined.

There were still no cars in sight, just tumbleweed and sage and a blue line of distant mountains in the fading afternoon.

While he relieved himself behind the Lincoln, she noted that his pants and shoes were still on the floorboard—and the keys were in the ignition.

Eddie Whitt heard the automatic door locks click shut.

"What you doin'?" he yelled, pounding on the air-tight windows. But he already knew his mistake, and a definite pleading had crept into his tone.

When she started the motor, he was begging.

"I ain't even got my shorts on! Gimme my pants! Throw my clothes out a window! Stuff 'em out! Just open the window a crack and stuff 'em out!"

As she drove away, she wondered if anyone would ever stop to help him. He looked forlorn and crazy: a tired salesman dressed only in his coat, shirt, and tie, standing in the middle of absolutely nothing.

In three hours, she was in Phoenix eating her first regular meal since that night in Amarillo. The wallet in Eddie Whitt's trousers had contained only $200, but she took it without a second thought; as for the car, she worried about driving it hot, so she parked it at the airport where she bought a ticket for Los Angeles. For an hour, she stood on the observation deck watching the airliners come and go and counting her disasters and blessings: she still had her luggage, she had come across the continent, she had survived.

That trip to the Coast, as she would always say afterward, was a rough road all the way—with something of a flourish at the end.

Of course, the movie business wasn't what she had hoped. It wasn't even in existence, exactly, so that its offices were in one place or so that it had any real definition. The streets of Hollywood, Burbank, Studio City, L.A., Westwood, and all the others blended together in a confusion of freeways and side roads. A producer at one studio had offices, she discovered, at another studio, too. Agents lied to her and wanted cash down payments for their services. A model/actress placement agency took her photograph for "the big production book all the stars are in" and charged her ninety dollars for the service—which, in turn, didn't get her into that book they showed her.

Once she had a lunch date with a producer, which had been arranged by a dyke agent she met at a party. A limo picked her up at her apartment just off Third Street in Beverly Hills, and the chauffeur drove her out to Burbank Studio. The gate man touched the rim of his cap when he bent down to say hello; then the chauffeur followed a blue line painted on the studio pavement, turning this way and that among old sets and sound stages until she was delivered to a brown brick and glass building. She wore a raw silk dress.

"Can we get this over as quick as possible?" the producer asked her.

"Aren't we going to lunch? I'm hungry," she complained.

"We both know what the other wants," the man said. "I'm gonna consider you for future projects, and you're gonna lie down on my desk."

"I wanted lunch at the studio commissary," Sally persisted.

"Okay, after," the producer conceded with a deep sigh.

His office was done in rich walnut with paisley drapes; on the walls were awards, plaques, and photographs of his children and wife; the rug was deep and soft. He had silver hair, an Italian name, and garlic breath, which made Sally wonder if he had already eaten lunch. On top of his desk—with only a new blotter for comfort—her raw silk dress whispered as they moved.

At the commissary, while she ate a crabmeat salad, he moved among the other tables, laughing and talking with important people whom she had never seen on the screen in a movie. But at a far table where the producer didn't go sat George Segal with two men, all of them smoking long, dark cigars.

This visit to the Burbank Studio commissary turned out to be Sally's biggest achievement in the movie business. A week later, she was drifting into daytime waitress jobs, long hours before her television set in the little apartment she couldn't easily afford, and days of hopeless hope.

She saved money for an airline ticket back to Philadelphia, hoping to see her mother—her father had died that year, alcoholic and bitter—but the money was spent, and she finally accepted a ride with a stuntman named Tooker who said he was going back to Denver in his jeep. She estimated Tooker's age as possibly younger than her own, so she figured he had come out to Hollywood with plans to throw himself off things for money but, like her, had given up the game.

"Yeah, that's about it," he allowed. "Gotta go home."

The jeep was a hard ride, but Tooker, at long

last, was shy. They drove across the desert and into the mountains eating store-bought cookies and talking about their lives. Sally seemed to have exhausted her supply of lies, so she told partial truths. Tooker talked a long time before mentioning his ranch.

"You got a ranch?"

"At Evergreen. Up in the mountains west of Denver."

"Evergreen," she said, pronouncing the word.

"Only got four horses," Tooker said as if apologizing. "But I got a pretty good apartment off Colfax Avenue in town. You're welcome to stay at either place, Sally, until you get yourself together."

"I'm as together as ever," she admitted.

"There's an A-frame on the ranch," he told her. "Just has one room, but there's a view of the meadow and creek. When I'm home, I leave the jeep up at Evergreen and drive another car, so you can keep this."

She thought Tooker was the sweetest person she had ever known. In a way, she wanted to sleep with him and hold him, but he made not the slightest overture even when she brought up the subjects of girls and sex.

"Are you gay?" she finally asked him, taking a chance.

"There's this street in Denver," he explained. "Colfax Avenue. There's a certain two or three block area along it—not too defined, actually—where the cowboy world bumps up against the gay neighborhood. The gays have this movie house that shows the same favorite gay films every weekend. The cowboys have their bars with Coors signs in neon on the windows. But in between is this area where the two life-styles blend. I think—in my soul—I belong right in that area, right in that little three-block stretch like nowhere else on the planet. I don't know if that's an answer or not."

"Well, I'd like to meet you some night when you've got your spurs on," Sally said, telling him how much she loved him.

She tried staying with Tooker, but nothing worked. Her two days at the A-frame up at Evergreen almost drove her crazy. "Cabin fever," Tooker told her. "And you sure did get it fast." In Denver, although there were bright lights and bars, she felt badly out of place, aching to get back East.

Tooker bought her steaks, tried to keep her cheered up, and finally gave her money for a flight home.

"The money don't mean nothing to me," he explained in his best drawl. "I always had money. I've had condos, Alfa Romeos, trips to London, and bigger ranches than the one I've got now. You take this and don't ever look back."

"I seem to be going the wrong direction," she said. "When I was heading West, I had hope. Now I'm going back, but I don't know what for."

"Maybe you should turn around again. If you give the movie business another shot, maybe you'll make it."

"You've probably changed my luck," she admitted. "Maybe I should go back again. But I'll go home, visit my mama, and see what happens."

He pressed the money into her hands.

And what happened, ultimately, was the same cycle: the same yearnings, the same struggle, the same eventual dependence on her body and looks to get by. It had all been the same, she felt, up until that night Jack Luce pulled her out of that underwater trap. The same: whore and wanderer.

Now, sitting in the apartment from which she had fled, her clothes back in the drawers, her scruffed luggage sitting at the foot of the bed, she had to think—with her usual capacity to hope for the best—that Jack Luce was right. Their lovemaking had been the best ever. He had asked her to help, so he needed her. Like Tooker and very few other men, he was strong enough to be tender with her. He had also saved her life, so she felt she owed him.

Yet she remembered the pain of that trip West years ago.

Deep inside herself, she was still on that journey. And, in spite of all, she still had hope—constant and blatant hope—that something or someone could be found.

# 9

Late in the day, Jack got a phone call from Norris at the film lab informing him that the blowups of the photos were ready.

"They came out all right?" Jack asked him.

"You'd never know these came from shots taken of magazine photos," Norris told him. "Remember me when you're doing somebody favors."

After picking up the photos, Jack drove back over to Sam's offices and editing rooms above the old cinema. The rooms smelled like stale cigarettes and cheap face powder. Carrying a Thermos of hot coffee, Jack set about the tiresome business of getting his sound reel of that fatal car crash.

First, he dubbed his sound tape on to 16 mm. sprocketed tape. Then he sat down at the editing table to create a frame-by-frame sync between pictures and sound, matching, at first, the sound and action of the car smashing into the street lamp. Next, he put the picture and sound track together in a Moviola and ran them. Carefully, he studied his result.

It worked. Better than he had anticipated.

Getting excited, he ran the strip again and watched, especially that moment before the tire exploded.

He stopped the Moviola, and there, in the freeze-frame shot, toward the top of the picture in a clump of trees, was a small flash of light surrounded by a haze —perhaps white smoke. The gunshot.

Jack poured himself a half cup of coffee, sipped at it, and spoke to the silent room around him. "That's it," he said.

Yet, making sure, he ran the filmstrip over and

70

over, watching that flash at the top of the photostrip and listening to the accompanying sound of the gun- shot.

At two o'clock in the morning, he shut down the editing room and drove back to his apartment with a final precaution in mind. Standing on a chair, he re- moved one of the acoustical tiles from the ceiling over his tape library. With some black electrician's tape he secured all his evidence to some water pipes beyond his false ceiling, then replaced the tiles. Everything was up there safe: the original sound tape, the photos and the subsequent filmstrip Norris had devised from them, and the final print with its new, added soundtrack.

Toward morning, thinking of what he had to do next, he sprawled on those sheets and pillows in the corner. Sally's soapy scent was on his bed, so he wanted to call her on the phone, but in the moment he resisted the urge he fell asleep.

He awoke the next morning to the voice and sounds of the Liberty Bell hawker, a crazy street musician who showed up here and there in the old neighborhoods for the tourists in town. This morning, the man was bopping and loudly singing beneath Jack's window while a crowd of kids laughed and called to him. For five minutes or more, Jack watched them down there on the street from his studio window. The sun was out, and everything seemed normal: traf- fic horns, barges, bells, all the familiar and reassuring noises.

As he left his building, he carried his tape record- er, a can of tape, and the mounted photos from the magazine. The Liberty Bell hawker, carried away with his performance, as usual, still entertained the kids on the block. The hawker had a high, distinct voice that Jack recalled having heard for years in ballparks, around Independence Square, and around the play- grounds.

Three blocks away Jack cut through a parking lot toward the police headquarters. An hour later, he was shown upstairs, led into an office, and given an uncom- fortable chair in the office of Detective John Mackey. During the long wait for Mackey, Jack took out the

71

single photo of the gunshot and set up his tape recorder on the corner of the man's desk.

When Mackay finally came in, he seemed immediately hostile.

"You think I don't remember you, Luce, but I do," the detective said. He was a burly, middle-aged man with a weary face. He had a habit of picking at his fingernails with a one-handed style, making the nails click slightly as if he were snapping his fingers.

"Where do you know me from?" Jack asked him, trying a smile.

"From the Keen Commission where you worked for a bunch of men who thought they were finding bad apples."

"I don't remember you," Jack managed.

"Yeah, but I thought it was you, so I found a file," the detective said. "You probably don't remember Freddie Corso, but you should."

"Of course, I remember," Jack replied.

"So I remember you, too, and don't like you and ain't inclined to help you. So what the hell do you want, and make it quick."

Jack sat there for a moment trying to consider alternatives, but there weren't any. Detective Mackey, at present, was heading the investigation into McRyan's death and helping to form a special commission.

"I came about McRyan's death," he began. "I brought some sound tape and a photo, and what I've got is just a sample of the positive proof I can show you or any commission."

"Proof of what?" Mackey snapped. He made the noise with his fingernails in clear agitation.

"Proof that McRyan was assassinated. Our governor was killed."

"Oh, I love conspiracy nuts. Fine, just fine."

"I've brought in a sample for you. A sound sample and a photo," Jack said, trying to continue.

"I wish I had a dime for every conspiracy theory I've ever heard. I could buy myself the whole state of Florida and go into early retirement."

"In this photo," Jack said, holding it up so that Mackey could see, "there's a flash and some smoke.

The picture was published right in *News Today,* but nobody seemed to notice. But that's not all—"

"I can't believe I'm hearing this. And not from an asshole kid who worked with the Keen Commission."

"Look at this flash and smoke," Jack insisted.

"That could be anything," Mackey said, glancing at the picture. "It could be a doctored photo! And why does everything have to be a conspiracy? A guy wins a tough primary, has too many drinks to celebrate, then drives off a bridge. A plain and simple accident!"

"But it wasn't. The tire was shot out. I heard it and recorded it."

"So you're an *ear*witness to the assassination? Hey, I like it. It has a nice ring."

"You're heading the investigation right now," Jack argued. "Have you checked that rear tire on McRyan's car?"

"Why should I?"

"Because it probably has a bullet hole in it. Because McRyan was killed and I saw and heard it."

"The special commisson we got forming will say it's an accident," the detective replied.

"But they haven't seen the evidence! They haven't heard my tape! I was there!"

"The guy who used to work for the Keen Commission was there!"

"If you refuse to listen to this material—on any grounds—you'll be making a big mistake, Mackey, because someone else up the line *will* listen," Jack said, and as he threatened the big detective, he began gathering up his recorder and tape. Mackey watched him for a moment, then put his hand across the desk and accepted the tape.

"Okay, I'll do my job," he said. "I'll run this crap down to the lab and see what they have to say."

"I'll go with you," Jack offered.

"No, you'll stay here—because I don't want you telling our men what they're hearing. I want them to hear it for themselves."

Jack gave him the tape. "If we could get the original film from which the magazine photos were made, you'd see that flash and smoke a lot clearer," he told Mackey.

"Karp's disappeared," Detective Mackey said. "He's selling his pictures to magazines, and we'll be lucky if we ever get copies."

"He's got to give you the pictures as evidence, hasn't he?"

"If we can find him."

"He could answer a lot of questions. Like what he was really doing out there with his camera. It's just too much of a coincidence for me that I was there working in the park that night and that somewhere close where I couldn't even see him was some punk photographer."

"I don't want to hear all your damned theories," Mackey said, and he started out with the tape.

"Just listen to the two sounds on that tape," Jack said. "The gunshot, then the blow out. Just listen to it with your police experts."

"This wasn't no political assassination," the detective said with full confidence. "There weren't any right-wing terrorists or Communist spies. Save your paranoia for public television. But I'll check this stuff out and get back to you."

He went out the door, and for a few minutes Jack sat in the uncomfortable chair at the detective's desk. Then he picked up the phone and asked the police switchboard operator to get him an outside line.

Sally's phone rang and rang.

A tiny wave of anxiety pulsed in his blood when she didn't answer.

After this, he phoned Sam just to check in.

"Where the hell you been?" the producer wanted to know. "We got a work schedule, and I'm doin' your job."

"How's that?" Jack asked.

"I'm auditioning screamers."

"Tell me that again. I love it."

"It ain't funny. It's hard work havin' these three girls in the sound booth all day," Sam complained. "Why ain't you here?"

"You'll get your effects. How long you been workin' with those screamers?" Jack gazed out of Detective Mackey's office into a wall of skyscrapers.

Across the way a window washer lowered his scaffold.

"I got a girl screamin' while another one pulls her hair. Maybe I'm gettin' somewhere, I don't know. I need you to help decide."

Jack repressed a laugh. "I'll be over later today," he promised.

"Debby's got messages for you," Sam said. "I'm switchin' you back to her phone." Jack waited while the line clicked and buzzed; then Debby, their buxom little receptionist, fumbled the phone to her face, breathed heavily, and managed to ask what he wanted. The messages, she finally told him, were from somebody named Sally and a man who said Jack wanted him to do some work.

"Was the man named Norris?"

"No, something else. I gave him your studio number," Debby sighed.

"And what about Sally? She leave a message?"

"Said she'd get in touch later in the day."

"That's all?"

"Who's Sally? New girl friend?"

Jack hung up the phone and stood in the middle of Mackey's office, that little tremor of worry going through him again.

After a minute, Mackey came back in, circled his desk, and leveled a look at Jack. "What the hell you trying to pull?" he asked.

"What do you mean?"

"The tape's got nothing on it," Mackey told him.

Incredulous, Jack took the tape and threaded it back into the recorder he had brought with him. Only a steady hissing noise came out of the machine. As Jack struggled to understand, he said, "Erased. This was my original tape I made out on Wissahickon Drive, but it's been erased."

"You came in here and talked all that assassination crap, then gave me a blank tape," Mackey said evenly.

"Somebody in your lab erased it," Jack said, trying to understand.

"Get out of here, Luce. You're nuts."

"You erased the tape I gave you!"

"Luce," the detective said, leveling a stare across the desk. "If you don't leave, I'm gonna have you arrested. Don't ask the charge."

"I had that tape last night and made a copy," Jack said, speaking before he thought about what he was admitting.

"Get out," the detective repeated. "And tell somebody else your story."

By the time Jack reached the street again, he felt like a complete fool. The recorder felt like dead weight, and he wasn't thinking too clearly.

He took a cab back to his studio and went upstairs. Everything had been ransacked: his tape library in disarray, chairs turned over, even those pillows on his bed cut open and searched. Suddenly filled with paranoia, he kept himself from looking up at the ceiling where he had hidden his materials behind the acoustical tile—as if someone might still be watching.

His first thought was that the police, tipped off by Detective Mackey, might have done it. But why? And who else could it be? Was McRyan such a threat that a whole ordered political and police establishment had to knock him off? Was it the governor's political rivals, his own lieutenants, someone like the efficient Lawrence Henry?

One thing was clear: whoever got McRyan was involved, now, in a monstrous cover-up and knew about the sound tape. The next logical step was clear, too: if they would go to this extreme to get rid of a piece of ambiguous evidence, surely they'd kill whoever threatened.

The receptionist said that someone called to whom she gave Jack's address. Would the police do that? No, they'd know his address.

In a corner of his forebrain, he was worried about Sally.

As all these concerns swam around in him, he paced around his studio feeling vulnerable and helpless. His work had been violated. Someone had fixed his best sound mixer forever; it looked as though it had been attacked with an ice pick. Boxes of tapes were open and strewn around, cut into ribbons and piled up in a wastebasket where some of them had been hurriedly burned. His whole library was in a shambles.

He pulled the chair over, stood on it, and opened the acoustical tile again. The filmstrip with its telltale soundtrack was still taped to the water pipes across the top of his ceiling, but this wasn't absolute proof now because the original tape was gone, and any expert could assert that Jack had manufactured this remaining evidence.

Only he knew. He took the material down, sat in the chair, held the evidence in his hands, and waited. Certainty had become compulsion, but he didn't know what his first move should be.

The phone rang, and he smiled as he heard Sally's voice.

"Where you been?" he asked her, relieved.

"Out. You been calling me?"

"I want you to see a piece of film—with my sound on it," he told her. "Will you stay there until I come over?"

"Yeah, I guess so."

"Is your roommate with you?" he asked, trying not to sound alarmed.

"Sure, she's here," Sally replied. "What's wrong?"

"Both of you stay there," he said. "I'm going by the office; then I'll come over. It's important. Just stay where you are."

# 10

Jack went back over to Sam's offices to pick up a projector so he could show Sally the filmstrip, but waiting for him there was the young television news reporter, Frank Donahue, who had a reputation in Philadelphia as a tough investigative type. Donahue wore a three-button suit, an almost permanent smile, and rings on his fingers, but his eyes revealed a quick intelligence. He was like a sharp kid dressed up to play the role of a gambler, Jack thought.

"I wonder if you've got a couple of minutes you could spare?" Donahue asked. They were standing at Debby's desk out front, and she gazed up at the reporter with the full admiration one gives a celebrity.

"Sure, why not?" Jack replied.

"Could we get to someplace private?"

They walked back along the corridor to the animation room where those postersized faces of Greta Garbo and Clara Bow smiled down on them from the walls. Donahue picked some lint off his suit as if Sam's untidy rooms might contaminate him.

"I don't have a lot of time, and I know you're in a hurry, so I'll get to the point," Donahue began, his smile intact. "You've been questioned by the police. And I feel a little awkward approaching you at this time, but I wouldn't be a competent newsman if I didn't ask you a few things outright. Jack, you told the police that somebody shot out the tire on Governor McRyan's car."

"Who told you that?" Jack asked him.

"I've got my sources."

"I went to the police since telling them that," Jack revealed. "I got called a conspiracy freak."

"I'm here, Jack, because I believe what I've heard you say, because I've looked into this thing myself and a hell of a lot doesn't add up."

"Like what?"

"Like the girl. Everyone pretends she wasn't in the car, but you saw her, didn't you?"

"You got good sources," Jack answered.

"I also understand that you've recorded the gunshot. I'd like to hear that recording, Jack. Could I hear it?"

"What for? Some sounds on a tape aren't going to mean anything," Jack said. "I've got a studio at home and a little sound lab here, and I could manufacture any sound, couldn't I?"

"You could, but I don't think you did," Donahue said. "You were talking about the girl and the events of that night before you had any chance to pull something. I figure you have the real thing. So let me put the tape on the air. You can say what you saw and heard that night. We play the tape for the TV audience."

"Nobody is going to believe a few loud sounds on a tape," Jack argued.

"I'm going to believe it," Donahue promised. "And I've got a way of making millions of viewers believe me."

"I saw you interview Manny Karp. Did you believe him?"

"No, Jack, I didn't. He's cheap and so wrong that I began to feel other things might be wrong with McRyan's case."

Jack studied the fancy young reporter, trying to decide if this might be the best course of action. The police couldn't be trusted and certainly wouldn't trust him. McRyan's friends and enemies couldn't be differentiated. And the idea of going on a popular television show would have the effect, at least, of giving him so much exposure that a kind of protection would be provided by it.

"I'd actually be safer if I did this," Jack said, thinking out loud.

"That's right. Get everything out in the sunlight. If you stay back in the shadows, someone can deal with you in the dark," Donahue warned.

"I can't decide," Jack said.

"If it's money that's keeping you from deciding, don't worry about it," Donahue said. "This could be the hottest story in the country right now. The sky's the limit. My people are in a position to pay—anything."

"Big money, huh?"

"No problem, Jack; you name it. My people will take care of it."

"I'm just interested in what sort of money we're talking about," Jack went on, leading the reporter.

"We're talking about the price you name. Whatever it is."

"I saw a man get killed," Jack explained carefully. "I saw a governor killed who was known to be tough and honest and who could possibly have been president. I want to know why and who. I want to know who busted into my place this morning. Because people aren't supposed to kill people in this country and get away with it. There aren't suposed to *be* political assassinations here. Not in this country. But I saw one! And I've got evidence on it!"

"Whatever your price—"

"I'm not talking about money," Jack said, trying to be understood.

"Look, I believe all those fine things myself," Donahue argued, sounding somehow all the more phony as he insisted. "But, Jack, you sell sounds, don't you? You *sell* your material. You sold it to the Keen Commission once, and now you'll do it again, won't you?"

"The gunshot isn't for sale," Jack told him.

"Here, take my card. Think things over, then call me at my studio," Donahue said. "If you think about things, you'll phone me."

"I can't talk anymore. I've got an appointment," Jack said, thinking of Sally.

"Just call me," Donahue went on, moving his rings up and down on his fingers. All in all, Jack thought, the guy was an unlovable type.

They walked back down the corridor. Debby, ever conscious of an opportunity to make an impression, batted her eyes as if she needed glasses.

"You need my help, Jack, you really do," Donahue was saying.

"But I don't need a negotiation. I'm not Manny Karp. And what I need most is someone I can trust," Jack pointed out.

"Tell me exactly what you've got, Jack, will you? How many minutes of tape? You've got the gunshot clearly, right?"

"No more," Jack said as he kept walking. "Not right now." He left Donahue standing in that crowded foyer beside Debby's desk.

"What's wrong with him?" Debby asked, breathing heavily and trying to place the profile of her breasts within Donahue's line of vision.

"Let him go," the reporter said. "He'll come back. When a guy names his price, he always does."

As Jack set up his film projector that evening,

Judy Demming, Sally's roommate, put on her coat and gloves. "You two have fun," she said cheerily as she moved toward the door. She was a small brunette whose wide lips gleamed with frosted lipstick.

"Stay if you want to," Jack offered weakly.

"No, I think you're going to show each other dirty movies," she said as she opened the door and went out. "Nothing kinky for me." They all laughed as they said their good-bys. Sally brought a tray of drinks and cookies from the kitchen; her mood was nervously pleasant, slightly giddy, as if this were a very important date, but Jack was all business.

She settled on the couch beside him, pulling her legs underneath herself and giving him a smile.

"I don't think you're going to like this," he warned her.

"I like you being here."

"Sally, I'm serious. Watch this carefully."

He switched off the lights, and the projector flickered into life at regular speed as Sally watched.

"Now I'm going to run it again," he told her afterward.

She was already somber as he reversed the film, stopped the machine, then started it again in slow motion. "I saw and heard it," she whispered. "I see what you mean."

In slow motion, the gunshot was bold and clear: the flash from the bushes, the noise, smoke, everything. Somehow, more than ever, the filmstrip seemed vivid and unmistakeable.

"Now that I see this," Sally said, "I remember. I heard the gunshot, too. Just before the tire blew out. And you took this to the police?"

Jack nodded. "They took my copy to their lab and brought me back a blank. Somebody erased it."

"You're sure?"

"I transferred it myself. I heard it played back. And while I was at the police headquarters, somebody got into my studio and ruined hundreds of tapes out of my library. They were looking for this."

"It's all perfectly clear—a gunshot! Picture and sound! If you show this to the right people, they'll understand, won't they?"

"What I have here could've been manufactured in a studio," Jack explained. "That's what they'd say, and they'd be right. And, besides, I don't know who the right people are! The police are mixed up in this. Everybody wants McRyan to sink without a trace. Nobody wants to know about you, the gunshot, a plot, anything."

"So what are you going to do?"

"What are *we* going to do, you mean? You were in that car. You're mixed up in it. It was arranged for you to be in that car—don't you see?"

"What do you know exactly?" she asked, getting uncomfortable.

"I can guess just about everything. You and Karp were setting up McRyan to be blackmailed—like lots of other Karp customers."

"Who told you something like that?" she asked, pouting.

"Sally, I got a look at some of your earlier work with Karp. Candid camera work at some seedy motel. Somebody was paying you to be with McRyan."

She left the couch and stood by a window, looking out, not wanting him to know about this, hating both him and herself.

"I wasn't in the car," she said, defensively. "Nothing's mentioned in the newspapers. I can deny it."

"The cover-up won't last," Jack told her. "I talked to a reporter who seems to know everything. We can't just disappear now."

"I can," she said. "I can get the hell down to Florida, as I wanted to do."

"Sally, listen to me," he said, going over to her. He put a hand on her shoulder, but she turned from him. "They want you to disappear permanently. I'm afraid for you. Hell, I'm afraid for myself."

"What's that supposed to mean?"

"Didn't I meet you in a car wreck ten feet underwater?"

"It was an accident," she said, double-checking herself even as she managed to get the words out. "Manny didn't know that some guy—" Her thoughts and memories were tripping along. "He didn't know somebody was going to shoot out the tire, did he?" Her voice, less convinced now, rose into a question.

"Sally, if I hadn't been there to pull you out of that car, you'd be dead now. They expected you to die." He waited for this to sink in, watching her face.

She gazed out that window as if something important out there demanded her attention, as if by giving the horizon her elaborate concentration all else would go away. Then, in a weak, small, hurt voice, she began to speak again.

"It was just another job," she managed. "Like the others. I'd get them into bed, and Manny would get everything on film. Husbands, city officials, mostly small-town guys who would always pay. And it was always for the money—some really dirty bucks."

"You needed money that bad?" he asked. The question sounded harsh, he realized, but there it was.

"Oh, god, Jack." She sighed, still gazing outside. "I'm still behind the makeup counter at Korvettes. I've been with so many guys, so many places, and betrayed and kicked in all of them."

"So you worked for Manny Karp?"

"Manny said it served the victims right. If they got caught, they deserved it. At first, yeah, putting those guys in a frame gave me some satisfaction."

"What about McRyan?"

"Same thing. I went to the Liberty Ball, met him, and we decided to leave together early." She sounded tough and unattractive revealing these things, but unable to hold back, she stumbled along, the words hurting both of them now. "We slipped out to his car early in the evening. I had two strong feelings: that I was with somebody very important and impressive and that this was just another mark, somebody stupid enough to get caught."

"Sally, I know it hurts to talk about all this, but do you know who hired Manny to get those pictures."

"No, I don't know. I never wanted to know."

"And don't you think Manny knew his client meant to shoot out the tire?"

"Once I got a feeling—just a hint—that something different might happen. But nothing firm."

"Oh, Sally." Jack sighed with disgust.

"I know Manny wouldn't do anything like that to me on purpose," she said.

"Don't act innocent in this," he warned her, "not after all you've been through! Try to see what's happening!"

"I got paid," she argued weakly.

"They risked your life," he told her. "They either thought you'd surely get killed—or at least risked your life."

Sally paced around the room. Jack's argument suddenly sank in, and she felt like a fool. What was inside her, she wondered, that had prevented her from seeing this? Why did she ever think of herself as an accomplice when she was just another victim all the time?

"Sally, we're both in trouble. Listen to me. You know too much, and so do I. There's no reason on earth why both of us should still be alive."

"If you're meaning to scare me, you're doing a good job," she answered.

"I've been made to look like a fool, but they're not going to be happy with that if I persist. No way they're going to let you off. So you're going to help us—both me and yourself. You're going to help me get that original film from Manny Karp. I need the original. Because if we don't get this out—on television for everybody in the country to see—they're going to close the book on us."

"Nobody knows where Manny is."

"We've got to find him and get that film." Jack told her. He took her face in his hands and made her look into his eyes.

"I think I believe you," she said in a whisper.

"You'd better. I'm worried about you, not just myself."

"You mean that?"

"Yeah, I do. But, believe me, somebody out there only wants to do us harm."

# 11

Somebody was there.

His name was Burke, and his background was a mixture: employment as a bodyguard, service in the military, where he often got into trouble, loyalties to assorted right-wing causes and groups, and a long criminal record.

In a way, he was too intelligent for the physical work that he inevitably did. He had an executive capacity for thinking about the long-term view of things, but he was cursed with the body of a giant, and liked violence, so that the dirty jobs always became his.

His first assignment in the McRyan matter was at the city garage just days after the car had been pulled from Wissahickon Creek. Some violence might have been required, but Burke had cleverly waited around, learning the habits and working hours of the men who watched the impounded autos; then he had simply gone inside to do his work.

Once, when a garage attendant strolled into the area where Burke stood in the shadows, Burke uncoiled the wire from his watch band and waited. The wire made a grating sound—a noise recorded on Jack's equipment that night when McRyan died—and then snapped back out of view when the attendant passed.

From his own car inside the public parking area of the garage, Burke took a used tire of the right size and rolled it along a ramp. He carried a crowbar. Even as he performed this act, he revealed his great physical capacity. He was like a rhino: powerfully built, somewhat awkward looking, but endowed with speed and a curious grace in movement.

At a metal door, he stopped, inserted the crowbar, and in one quick movement tore it open.

The remains of McRyan's car stood at the far end of the impounding area. A shaft of pale sunlight slanted through a window just beside it, lighting Burke's efforts as he knelt down and began work. He ran his fingers around the tire on the car, making sure; near the rim of the bottom edge was a small hole, as he expected. Moving quickly, he used the flattened edge of the crowbar as a tire tool and opened the hubcap. In only minutes, he had changed tires and had rolled the incriminating evidence back outside, along the ramp, toward his personal car where it was locked away safely in the trunk.

The noontime activity had taken, in all, twenty minutes. He drove out of the public garage, smiled at the gatekeeper as he paid, and pulled into the traffic near city hall. Intelligence, speed, strength, a little daring—no one would be the wiser except a few ignorant garage attendants who would wonder why someone might have pried open that metal door leading into a room of smashed-up cars.

Burke drove out Charlestown Road toward a special Japanese restaurant he liked. There he had a drink and walked in the gardens before dining. By one o'clock, he was seated at the steam table, watching his favorite cook spin the sharp-bladed knives and fix the meal. Of all Burke's pleasures, good dining ranked highest. He had eaten enough prison food in his life; now his money and spare time were spent at gourmet restaurants or in special places like this where the serenity and service suited him.

"Excuse, please," a waiter other than his own said while he dined. "Are you by any chance Greg Ruzinski? If so, I would like autograph?"

The mistake had occurred before. "No, go away, please," Burke answered. He continued with his chopsticks as the man left. He did look something like Greg Luzinski, a burly outfielder for the Phillies baseball team, he admitted, but he hated to be interrupted at a meal.

And now, especially, he was thinking of his next assignments in the McRyan situation.

He might have been thinking of his whole life. He was a Jersey boy, raised in the tough Camden neighborhoods, and had tried to participate in sports on the football and wrestling teams, but he had always talked back to the coaches, had told them they were fools, and had invariably quit. In the military service, it was the same: Burke had been smart enough to be an officer but had contented himself with bucking authority. Finally, at a dirty little camp in Louisiana, a hotheaded captain had pulled a knife on Burke one night at a beer hall.

"Oh, sir, don't pull no knife on me," Burke said to the man.

"You big bastard. I'm gonna cut you open," the captain warned.

Burke had only smiled. He picked up a match book from the table where they had been sitting. Everyone in the room had frozen into silence.

"Sir, if you don't put down that knife, I'm going to fold this match book," Burke told the officer, "and then I'm going to kill you with it."

The color went out of the captain's face, but he somehow regained himself. The bartender searched for a .22 caliber pistol he had misplaced.

"Fuck your match book," the captain managed.

It was the last thing he said. Burke lunged, dodged the knife, and struck a blow to the man's throat.

He went to a Southern military prison where he became a virtual legend as an escape artist—punished more severely, of course, each time he was captured and returned. He once hid in a drainpipe for two days. Another time, he made arrangements to be picked up by a car outside the gates and ended up back in Camden where, on a visit to his mother, the authorities picked him up. That time, he was absent from the prison for nine weeks, but on another occasion, trying to hide in a garbage truck, he had been captured after only nine minutes of freedom.

His most extraordinary escape was on the river. The prison lay in the bend of the Mississippi, and on a warm spring day, as the swollen waters ripped along in a brown swirl, Burke set himself free, clinging to a dead log, and hoping for the best. He had a vague idea that he might float all the way to New Orleans—float right down Bourbon Street, perhaps, and into a fancy restaurant where he would order oysters and crêpes.

For two days he floated. Once he hid in a clump of willows where he could look downstream at guards on a bridge. They were posted and waiting, stopping cars that crossed and keeping the river in view, but he waited until dark, then passed underneath and continued on. The hours became dreams that he filled up with his hate. He wanted to kill every officer, policeman, and woman who had ever crossed his life. Women, especially—even his mother, who, he figured, had turned him in during that long escape that had taken him home. No girl friend, no wife, no kin, no stranger, no female acquaintence had ever done him anything except harm.

In the hour of his capture, a gull flew down and sat on the log with him. He was hungry, cold, dazed, and nearly delirious by this time, and the bird seemed out of place, as if it should be perched on some man's raft far out at sea rather than here on this mighty inland river. He wanted to talk to it, as if it were a demon, but he was too weary to speak. With his eyes half closed, he watched it until it faded and a sheriff in brown khakis lifted him into a rowboat.

Back at the prison, he stayed in solitary confinement again. Then, one day, he was released and taken before a new commandant, who offered him a cigarette and seemed unusually calm in Burke's threatening presence.

"You have a terrible record," the commandant said, "but a certain consistency. I want to ask you a few questions."

"Go ahead," Burke answered. The sunlight spilling into the office hurt his eyes but felt warm and good.

"Do you think you could follow orders if you received for your trouble some very nice rewards?"

"Maybe," Burke allowed, sucking on the cigarette.

"I believe you're still basically a good soldier—

perhaps one of the best of your breed," the commandant said.

"I'm a killer in my gut," Burke announced.

"That's what I mean. You'd do well in special forces even today. You have amazing instincts. I know of an organization outside the prison, at present, which could use your talents. But first we have to get you out of here."

"How do we do that?" Burke asked.

"You must serve a little more time, but I want you prepared to serve these friends of mine on the outside. They believe strongly in their country. They're not afraid of violence or direct methods."

"What are they prepared to do for me?"

"They will pay you well and treat you with respect," the commandant said. "In turn, you might be expected to take some very direct action, and you would always be expected to follow orders."

"I'd like to get out and have money," Burke agreed.

"Good. I want you to attend class with another inmate—a man skilled in karate techniques but also in the strong, political ideology some of us believe in. You can be as violent as you want with him, but that won't matter. You'll learn from him. And when you leave prison, I think you'll be even more special than you are now."

Burke did learn, and in three months he was out of prison and employed as a bodyguard for a wealthy and patriotic oil man from Arkansas. The oil man had a complicated divorce and flew to Pennsylvania each week to visit with his family; he also had enemies, deals, cars, houses, and strong political sentiments. Burke pleased his new employer, but when he accompanied the oil man on the trips to Pennsylvania, the ex-wife was too uneasy around him.

"Just don't bring him here," she told the oil man. "I can't help it, but I'm afraid of him."

"Why? Has he threatened you?" the oil man asked.

"He's a threat when he's standing around doing nothing," she replied, and the answer seemed to amuse the oil man a great deal, and he told Burke.

"You're not going to hurt her, are you?" he asked Burke, laughing.

"Not really. But I don't mind hurting women at all," Burke answered, his eyes flashing with malice.

Eventually, Burke learned a great deal about the oil man's political connections. Conversations flowed freely around the big bodyguard because it was assumed that he understood little, but, of course, everything was abundantly clear to him. One object of great concern was a Philadelphia politician named McRyan, a man with a moderate record who had secretly promised aid and support to a number of right-wing paramilitary groups that were dedicated to American aggressiveness. As McRyan's career flourished, as Burke understood things, he had defected; he had accepted a lot of money from the oil man and others but had forgotten their cause.

After a while, Burke also surmised that the politician McRyan might be sleeping with the oil man's ex-wife. This was confirmed one afternoon in summer beside the oil man's swimming pool out on Lake Catherine in the middle of Arkansas. They were drinking frozen daiquiris when the oil man suddenly announced, "I just know my ex-wife is sleeping with that politician back East and I want to kill either one or both of them. Which do you think I should kill, Burke?"

"I don't have any opinion," the bodyguard answered tactfully.

"Well, dammit, I want to kill somebody," the oil man snorted.

After that, their afternoon conversations around the pool or in the boat, where they often sat together bass fishing, turned to murder and assassination. The oil man mentioned Kennedy, Gandhi, King, and other famous men who had been shot down and sometimes asked Burke if he could manage such a job.

"I'm not much with rifles and long-range murder," Burke told him. "What I'd prefer is hand-to-hand activity."

"What about women? You once said you like to hurt 'em."

"Best of all," Burke answered.

As time went along, though, the wife was never mentioned as a victim, and the focus of the talks turned on the politician, who, as Burke saw things, was a safer target for the oil man and whose death, if it could be arranged, would make the oil man a great number of political friends.

"Any day now," the oil man began to promise.

"Ready when you are, sir," Burke would always reply.

But the day didn't arrive, and Burke left the employment of the oil man to become a special consultant to a secret organization in Florida, a paramilitary group that stored guns and dried foods all around the state at special sites. Burke thought this work dull and eventually said so. He fell into a series of arguments with his immediate superior, so the job ended.

After this, he went to work for a man with a large apartment on Fifth Avenue in New York, a man who gave Burke no particular duties. The man's name was Murray, and he provided Burke with a suite of nice rooms, gave him a check for one thousand dollars every Friday, and hinted that important duties would eventually arise.

"You've come to me with the highest recommendations," Mr. Murray always told Burke. "I know that when a mission comes, you'll be ready."

"Yes, sir, I will," Burke would always reply.

With time on his hands, a curious thing happened to Burke: he became, in turn, depressed and highly nervous. For a while, he drank heavily and developed a stomach ulcer, which was treated one night in the emergency room at Bellevue. After this, he stopped drinking, but things became worse. He sometimes stayed in his suite, the television picture on and the sound off, and wept. Then he took long walks all over Manhattan. The gourmet food he enjoyed in restaurants was his only normal pleasure; otherwise, he kept disjointed hours, sometimes not sleeping, and walked everywhere.

Six months after going to work for Mr. Murray, he killed his first victim.

She was a waitress in the Village. He simply followed her along Barrow Street one evening, pulled her into a doorway, and stabbed her a number of times with an ice pick, holding her in his arms as her life trembled away. For a few days afterward, he felt calmer, so much so that Mr. Murray remarked on it.

"Yes, sir, I do feel better," Burke admitted.

"Do you ever have a woman?" Mr. Murray asked him.

"Yes, sir, just the other evening," Burke replied, not being specific.

"A good man needs to satisfy himself occasionally," Mr. Murray philosophized.

Burke agreed.

He studied his employer's habits and found nothing of interest. The man seemed wealthy and idle. He read books, watched television, and went out in the evenings with friends. At first, his only conversations with Mr. Murray concerned the preparation of good foods, which both of them appreciated, but after a while they discussed their ideology.

"It is much better if the United States rules the world absolutely, don't you think so?" Mr. Murray asked.

"We have got to," Burke concurred. "We can't give it to godless Russia. We have to help the emerging, poor countries of Latin America and Africa. And we can't depend on the spineless and decadent nations of Europe."

"Burke, you amaze me with your insights," Mr. Murray said.

"Thank you, sir."

"That mission I have for you is very near. Do you have any idea what it is?"

"Perhaps. Is it in Philadelphia, by any chance?"

"Burke, you're truly an amazing person," Mr. Murray replied.

# 12

When he arrived in Philadelphia, Burke reported to Lawrence Henry, a powerful aide to a deceased governor—the governor, in fact, Burke imagined he would be assigned to kill. Henry was articulate, distinguished looking, cultured, and all the things Burke was not. From the beginning, neither man seemed to like the other, but they remained in contact daily.

At first, Burke was ordered to accomplish two simple jobs: he destroyed the tape library belonging to some sound technician, and he changed a tire at the police garage. These chores reminded him of the simple-minded efforts of the paramilitary group in Florida that spent time worrying over dried foods in airtight packages that could be squirreled away for the coming nuclear war.

"I don't like chores," he told Lawrence Henry.

"There will be other things for you," the aide replied.

"When? I'm anxious."

"If I hadn't received top references for you, I'd have you sent back to New York," Lawrence Henry snapped at him. "Be patient. An important man has been taken care of, and there are loose ends."

"The girl?" Burke asked hopefully.

"The less you know about matters, the better," Henry answered.

"I can take care of the girl."

"Yes, I know. But everything has to be coordinated."

During the next day, Burke's extreme nervousness returned. He wanted nothing to eat, no sleep, not even a single thought in his head. He hated Lawrence Henry and felt he should call Mr. Murray in New York or the

93

oil man in Arkansas and ask their permission to do things his own way. Confused, he took a few drinks at a bar on Race Street, but the whiskey burned his stomach and made him ill.

Then he prepared his silent, personal arsenal. He began to wear his ice pick in a small leather thong affixed to his belt; the wire was ready inside the fake Rolex on his wrist, coiled and deadly; deep in his coat pocket was a steel bar that he used to weight his fist; he even carried a large match book—which, in his mind, was a deadly weapon, too.

On his own, without any instructions from Lawrence Henry or anyone else, he began to watch Sally's apartment. He followed her on several of her excursions down into the run-down neighborhoods of old hotels and bars on the outskirts of Chinatown. She was obviously looking for someone, and he wished he knew who. He watched Sally's roommate, Judy Demming, and her boy friend, Jack Luce, who would also have to be killed, if he understood things rightly. If he were running this operation, he told himself, he would take care of everyone smoothly and quickly before matters got worse.

"What happened to the rifle expert who shot out McRyan's tire?" he asked Henry at one of their meetings.

"He was imported. A foreigner," Henry told him, "but that's none of your business. Now he's back where he came from."

"You should have played it safe and had him killed," Burke said.

"You'd have liked the job, right?"

"I wouldn't have minded. Much safer that way. The same for all these others you're worrying about."

"Don't be hasty," the aide warned him.

"I'm getting very nervous. I want to calm myself in my work."

"There's no reason we shouldn't kill everyone concerned, I suppose," Henry remarked. "Even you."

The conversation ended, and Burke complained no more, but Lawrence Henry, he felt, should have never said that.

On a cool night blanketed in fog, a taxi pulled up

in front of Sally's apartment, and the driver honked his horn. After a minute, Sally emerged wearing a dark jacket, her blonde hair flashing in the light of the street lamp as she stepped inside the taxi. As the taxi pulled away, Burke followed in his car.

The ride back across town was a confusing one. The fog, unusually heavy traffic, other taxis moving in and out, and Burke's own nervousness made tailing Sally's taxi difficult. Once, Burke was sure he had lost her. Then, finally, he felt sure she was going back to that seedy area on the streets bordering Chinatown and that in spite of all the confusion he was following the right taxi, after all.

A slow drizzle started.

Again, he lost her. In that same neighborhood where she had been going for the last two days, he pulled to a curb and stopped. He got out of his car, stood by its opened door, and peered down a street that smelled of cooked cabbage and rice. From somewhere near, a church bell sounded.

Then he saw her blonde hair.

He closed his car door and hurried down the block, falling in behind her. Nearing her, he watched her swaying walk as she moved through the light rain and fog; the roll of her hips made him remember the photographs Lawrence Henry had shown him—pictures of her naked and in bed. His hand moved to his fake Rolex and pulled out the wire.

An Oriental man, hurrying along in his rain slicker, an apron showing beneath it, bumped into Burke and slowed him down. "Sorry," the little man said, but Burke didn't reply.

At a corner, she stopped, paused, then turned in another direction. They were entering an empty street adjacent to an excavation site. A silent building crane rose up and disappeared into the fog and rain above their heads.

As they moved together, Burke closed the distance between them. Then, as if she meant to cooperate with her own murder, she conveniently crossed the street toward the excavation. He moved in behind her so that he could hear her quick footfall on the wet pavement.

Then he caught her. With one quick move, he looped the wire around her head and pulled her toward the excavation.

A flimsy barrier blocked their way, but he butted it aside with his hip and pulled her down into the soggy excavation pit in the empty street. A greasy mud covered them as they slid down toward the bottom, but although their progress was slow and wet, the wire was firmly around her neck so that she couldn't cry out.

She struggled, trying to reach behind her and grab him, but he was far too strong for her. He easily tightened the wire. One turn, two, three.

For several minutes, he pulled her against his body, feeling her quiver and die like a helpless bird. Her buttocks pressed against his thighs, and her perfume addled him. Then she slumped away, gone.

Muddy, his nerves singing, his mouth dry, he finally turned her lifeless body over so that he could see her face.

It wasn't Sally—the wrong one.

For a moment, he tried to gather his thoughts. His shoe rested in a pool of water, and wet mud soaked into his pants and announced itself coldly to his skin. The wire around her neck was still tight in his fingers, and the rain beat down softly in his eyes, and he couldn't think—the taxi and the fog, the same blonde hair and dark jacket, the confusions of Chinatown and the rain. It took him several minutes, lying at the bottom of that wet pit with his victim in his arms, to realize that neither Lawrence Henry nor anyone else would know of his mistake. *This was my own mission, after all,* he told himself, *and no one will ever be the wiser.*

He had killed for practice.

Meanwhile, less than a block away, Sally entered the Bond Hotel, its red neon sign sporting only two remaining letters. After a frantic two days, she had found the place where Manny Karp was hiding.

# 13

Searching for Manny was as if Sally had finally come to the ends of the earth, looking for herself. Now she entered the cheapest of cheap hotel rooms: sagging bed, rickety chairs and desk, a torn shade that occasionally glowed with those two red-neon letters hanging outside.

Around Manny's work area—where he had installed a photographic enlarger to make the negatives he was selling to magazines—there were ends of sandwiches, junk-food wrappers, empty cardboard coffee containers and soda bottles, and piles of dirty clothes. The enlarger was threaded with 16 mm. film—the end of the film resting in Manny's hands as Sally walked in.

"You look worn out, Manny," she said by way of hello.

"Sally. Come on in." He looked, in fact, too tired to move or to make excuses or to bend his face into any real recognition.

"Jesus, don't they ever clean this place?" she asked, looking around.

"Well, you gotta get up early to catch the maid. I ain't made it yet," he answered. "How'd you manage to find me?"

"There were just so many holes you'd crawl into," she said. "I went down our old list."

"Want a drink? Come on, take off your jacket."

"This isn't a social visit," she said. "And I ought to be mad. You almost got me killed the other night."

"Hey, I didn't know that was gonna happen that way." He went over to the rickety desk and poured himself a shot of Scotch in a MacDonald's cup. He seemed terribly nervous with her there; his hands shook, and his smile didn't work.

"You didn't bother to pull me out of the water," she said.

"I took off as soon as I saw that guy jump in the water after you! I mean, he did a hell of a good job—better'n I could've done! I don't know if I ever told you this, but I can't even swim, babe!"

"You're a beauty, Manny."

"I knew you was gonna be sore at me," he admitted, and before she could answer, he drank off his Scotch and tried to get his smile working once more.

Sally strolled around the room. It smelled like Manny: indefinably bad. At the torn window shade, she stopped and looked out at the fog.

"Have a drink, will ya?" he suggested, trying to make conversation.

"You know, I've been thinking about things," she said. "They just don't add up. Like, how did I end up in a car at the bottom of a creek—with the governor?"

"Guy had a blow out," Manny offered.

"Naw, Manny, somebody shot out the tire. You didn't hear that?"

"Who says? How'd you know that?"

"I just know, Manny. I got scientific proof."

"You know some scientist?"

"Manny, you and I are in big trouble. I want you to think about it. If you think about things real hard, you'll figure out that if they're willing to kill a popular governor, they're also willing to kill us. We are very small fish. We can just disappear."

"I didn't know nothin' about that rifle shot," Manny argued, revealing everything. "Still don't."

"Manny, you got to level with me," Sally told him.

"All I know is that some guy called me weeks ago, right? Says he's working for another candidate that's interested in getting McRyan framed. He sounds normal, and his scheme sounds normal. He's heard about our divorce work, he says, and that's the sort of thing he has in mind for the governor. Offers me six grand, so I say okay."

"Six? You told me three!"

"Well, yeah, three before and three after. I was gonna tell you."

"You were gonna tell me as I went down for the third time, I guess."

"Soon as I collected, I was gonna pay you. Don't you believe me?"

"Manny, no. But that doesn't matter. I'm here because you've got to help us now or things could get terrible."

Manny poured himself another drink, his eyes darting around the room as he thought fast and talked. "Look, he wasn't supposed to die," he said. "I was ready to take pictures of a little crackup. The police were set to come. They were gonna pull you outta the car with the governor, I was gonna take pictures, the guy's career was gonna take a nosedive. Simple. But the car swerved over, hit that lamppost, and went into the water! Christ!"

"I was floating around in McRyan's blood," she told him.

"He wasn't supposed to die."

"Maybe that's true, but we killed him," Sally said.

"We? We didn't do nothing! You were in the car, I was in the park, and somebody else shot out that tire! We didn't kill him! And, besides, no one is exactly crying over how things turned out. The guy's career was going to be finished. This way, he comes out ahead! He's a damn martyr! The legislature passed one of McRyan's bills this morning! The guy's a better politician dead than alive!"

"You're a pig, Manny, and that's a pig explanation. The governor was murdered—out and out. Tell you the truth, I'm scared, too."

"You better keep your mouth shut if you don't want to go to jail. We can both go up for fifty years if we start yellin' murder."

"It's not jail I'm scared of."

She was gazing out of the window again. As the fog lifted, she could see a giant building crane a block away—its awkward, black silhouette.

"Keep your mouth shut and keep your money," Manny said. "Babe, this is the biggest thing since the

Zapruder film. Maybe bigger. This is history and cold cash we got here. It's gonna be in every newspaper, magazine, and six o'clock news program on TV and radio. They're gonna build a TV special around this. Don't you understand? We got a fortune here."

She sat down on the rough chair beside the window. "Maybe you're right, Manny." She lied. "Maybe we should take the money and run."

"That's it. Get down to the tables in Atlantic City and blow a few. Go to the sun. You ever been to the Bahamas?"

"Maybe you're right. And maybe I'll have a drink and calm down."

"We could have a party right here tonight," Manny suggested.

"Maybe I should. To calm myself," she said, leading him on.

"Here, take this," he said, and he poured her four strong fingers of Scotch in a used Dixie cup. "Feel good."

"Would you get me some water to cut that?" she asked sweetly.

"Water? Yeah, sure, I'll step down the hall to the lavatory."

She already had matters figured out, so when he left the room with her whiskey, she moved quickly toward the enlarger, gathered up Manny's whole stack of negatives, and tucked them into a cardboard box that was handy. Her breath pounded hard, but she successfully got everything in the box and started out. She heard the water running in the tap as she turned down the stairway.

"Yeah, don't be a dope, babe," Manny was saying from the bathroom. "Money's money."

As she made the turn on the landing, she heard him come out of the bathroom and call after her. "Hey, hold it!" he called. "I got your whiskey!" By the time he returned to the room, of course, she was gone.

She was afraid to go back to her place immediately, so she arranged to meet Jack at his studio where they viewed Manny's original film—in color—off a blank wall above the hotplate. Jack had created a soundtrack, so they heard the two explosions distinctly; and this time, clearly, in the midst of the smoke in that telltale frame, there was something else.

"I think that's the barrel of a rifle," Sally said afterward.

"That's what it was," Jack agreed. "This is dynamite." After reversing the film, they ran it one more time.

"Now what?" Sally asked when he had switched off the projector.

"I think we only have one choice. I'm going to show it to that television reporter. I didn't like him, but he's hot for the story."

"Will I have to go on TV?" Sally asked, slumping in a chair. She seemed worn out, as if she barely had the strength to raise this small protest.

"It will be for your own protection," Jack told her. "I know you're tired. But, Sally, I don't think we can trust the cops or any of McRyan's own people in this. Let's go with Donahue. At least he's mercenary. And in what we're doing money is almost the cleanest thing around."

"I'm almost too tired to be scared anymore," she said.

"Don't be," Jack warned her. "It's funny, but I know we're being watched."

# 14

From the phone booth on the street outside Jack's apartment, he was being watched even as he said this. Burke was gazing up toward the window where Jack folded up the projector; the bodyguard had occupied the booth for more than twenty minutes, holding the phone to his mouth but talking to no one; the streets were empty at this late hour, but he felt strangely agitated and out of sorts. When his quarry moved away from the window again, he stepped out of the booth and departed. *No more tonight,* he told himself.

Back at his hotel, Burke could feel the wires snapping inside him; like that deadly little wire he wore on his wrist, his inner wires were taut and singing, breaking one by one under the strain. He lay down on his bed and fell asleep, but his dreams overpowered him. In one, that gull that had perched on the log with him came to perch on the bedpost; the bird had a cold eye, and in its beak it bore what seemed to be a strip of raw flesh. In another part of the dream, Burke was floating on a child's toy in the oil man's swimming pool, but the pool was like a river, endless and flowing, and eventually its current led underground into stark and hideous caverns.

Toward morning, Burke sat on the edge of his bed, his body damp and shivering, and tried to gather his thoughts for a meeting he had with Lawrence Henry before noon.

"Aren't you hungry?" Lawrence Henry asked him later. They were in a private suite at another hotel, dining on a gourmet room service. "I thought you liked good food?"

"I'm not feeling too well," Burke answered.

The soup was lobster bisque, the furniture around them was solid American colonial, and the silver was properly heavy, but Burke's hands rested on the plate before him like weights.

"You have a nervous condition, don't you?" Henry asked while he ate.

"I'll be all right."

"To tell you the truth, Burke, some of our people are concerned about you. The short of it is this: we're moving you out of the city and giving you a job someplace else."

"No, you're not," Burke answered.

"What's that?"

"You're not moving me anyplace. I'm going to do the job I was sent to do."

"Sorry, we've spoken to Mr. Murray in New

York. There seems to be agreement up and down the network."

"But I don't agree," Burke said. He stared into his empty plate.

"That hardly matters," Henry said, finishing his soup and opening another silver tureen that sat before them. "All of us are followers and leaders. McRyan was a leader, but he abandoned his true followers, and you see what it got him."

"Don't threaten me," Burke said.

"It's no threat. You understand this principle as well as any of us."

"What I understand is that few of you will take action. Listen, I know everything that's going on here and understand it, I believe, more than anyone else. I know the whole network. I know that certain individuals connected with the McRyan incident are very dangerous to us—simple people like a dumb whore and a sound technician. I know about you, Mr. Murray, people in Florida and Arkansas. And you know what I see? Procrastination and worry. Piddling activity—like survival schools in the event of nuclear war. I don't see anyone taking action against our enemies."

"I'm going to have to tell Mr. Murray about your—"

"Murray is a deadbeat," Burke interrupted. "He wears silk robes and goes out to dramas in Manhattan. If you bother me, I'll go to New York and kill Mr. Murray. I'll kill you. If you want me to be the bully, I will be. I'll take over this operation by assassination—the way all true revolutions have to begin."

Lawrence Henry had put down his silverware.

"I've had the status of a chauffeur," Burke said. "But no more."

"You're out of your mind," Henry said.

"I could kill you for saying that," Burke snarled, and for a moment he seemed ready to spring across the table at the frightened executive.

Lawrence Henry got up to put on his coat and leave.

"You won't be able to find me these next few days, so don't bother," Burke went on. "I'll be doing

103

the necessary work. After it's finished, you'll see that I've been right to accomplish things quickly and smoothly. You'll thank me for it. In any case, it will be too damned late."

"We should never have gotten mixed up with a criminal type like you," Henry sputtered as he put on his coat.

"You arranged McRyan's death, not me," Burke said. "And did a clumsy job which has left a number of loose ends. You're criminals, too. But that's all right. The means justify ends, at present, and a few heads have to roll. And I don't really mind doing the dirty work. I like it. But when it's finished, I won't be put back in the drawer until needed again. I'm one of you now, and when this job is finished, I'll tell you my needs."

"Tell us your needs?" Henry said with sarcasm.

"I want money, status, mobility, everything the rest of you enjoy. I want to handle things right because the rest of you seem to have forgotten how to."

"I'm going to phone Murray about you," Henry threatened.

"If you do, give him my message. Tell him that if he crosses me, I'll come to New York and kill him. Give yourself the same message."

"My god," Henry whispered.

"Get out of here," Burke told him.

At the end of the day, Burke checked into the Fairmont Hotel, then thought better of it and changed to an obscure new address on a side street. His nerves were rattling under his skin, and his head throbbed with such pain that once inside his room, he sat down, decided against going out to supper, and tried to gain control of himself. He thought about phoning the oil man in Little Rock in order to consolidate his bid for power but decided to wait until he had completed his tasks. Killing Mr. Murray, he also considered, should be a possibility—and Lawrence Henry, just to let everyone know who they dealt with.

But his headache stopped him. He lay on the bed with his fingers pressed against his temples.

When he closed his eyes, the mysterious gull returned, sitting on the bedspread beside him, mocking him.

# 15

During the night Jack slept with Sally, her body curled warmly into his, their heads propped up on those pillows that had been slit open during the search of his apartment, as if they needed reminders that they were involved at the edges of an intrigue that threatened them. After their lovemaking, he lay awake for a long time thinking about himself. He remembered his time at home with his mother, his army days, and went back over those curious months working for the Keen Commission one more time, Detective Mackey's accusations and doubts still ringing in his ears.

At nine o'clock the next morning, as Sally still slept in her deep exhaustion, Jack phoned Donahue. At first, he talked to secretaries, who passed his call along to other secretaries, then the reporter himself answered.

"It's Jack Luce," he said, reminding him. "I've been thinking about what you said."

"Oh, yeah, Jack, how are you?" Donahue asked, his voice sounding strangely distant.

"I've got Karp's original film, and I've rigged my sound to go with it. If you want to run them together, you'll see that McRyan's death was no accident. You'll see and hear the gunshot—clearly."

"Uh, Jack, I can't talk very well right now," Donahue replied. "Can we get back to each other later today? What's your number?"

Jack gave Donahue the information, agreed to stay close for the next contact, and hung up. Sally was still sound asleep, a bare arm thrown out at a graceful angle from the twisted sheets.

Was Donahue possibly involved in the conspiracy, too? Was that a stall on the phone? Jack began to speculate about just how far a conspiracy—and the McRyan matter definitely involved one—extended. The police, the politicians, newscasters: how far could a thing like that go? As he stood by the phone in his studio looking across the room at Sally's sleeping form, the questions kept coming. The terrible, dark, penetrating questions: how many circles, ring after deadly ring, in the pit of secret knowledge? Did everyone, possibly, inside the corridors of power already know? Was the stupid public kept stupid on purpose, as they were in the Kennedy and King assassinations? And was a man alone a fool to chase the truth when no one wanted it and when the object, all along, was to keep it hidden away?

*All one's life is an escape from certain truths and responsibilities,* Jack mused, *and certainly, in my own case, a big dose of reality was always something to be avoided. I retreated into my little technology,* he told himself. *I was a sound man in the way some musicians are hooked on their instruments.*

Jack's father had died tending a little tomato garden at the side of their house. Left alone with his mother, who was modestly well cared for, he tinkered with his equipment and built the beginnings of his tape library. In his room, alone, his headphones on, he shut out the world. Norris was his only good friend in those early days—and only because they were tinkerers together.

"I want you to go to the university," his mother scolded him.

"Later on. Maybe next spring," he told her.

His mother was often too much in the world to suit him; she dealt with money, loneliness, the grief of his father's loss, meals in the kitchen, all that. He sought his special cave deep in the drumming distances of new sounds. At his equipment, he experimented with electronic music for a while, grooving on the synthesizer. It was music that led him to Ivy Hatter, the pretty redheaded keyboard player.

She was an ex-Bryn Mawr student who worked part time at the Owl, a chic little used-book store over on Yarrow Street, and played nights with her own combo at the small clubs. She advertised in some of the offbeat newspapers for someone to teach her sounds on the synthesizer, so Jack showed up. Even her presence was an education for Jack: she wore nothing underneath her flimsy and peek-a-boo dresses, she smoked pot for breakfast, her talent was rampant and wonderful, and she had retreated into her own esthetic zone as obviously as Jack had retreated into his.

"So you move this lever up and down—up for the higher sounds and down for the bass notes?" she asked, leaning over his console. The blouse fell away from her breasts, and her smell was like apples and clove.

"Yeah," he managed.

"What's the matter?"

"Nothing. You got it right. Now this knob over here—"

"Do I bother you?" she asked without the slightest coyness.

"Sure. You bother me a lot."

"Sexually?"

He took a long look at her, fixing his eyes in hers. "Yeah," he said, thinking all the while that she was simply the most beautiful thing he had ever met.

"We got a lot of work to do," she told him, her voice dropping an octave. "If you're going to be distracted, maybe we should go ahead and fuck."

"Right now?" he asked.

"Sure, take off your clothes."

He was not inexperienced, yet he was. His girls had been high school coeds groped in the rear seats of musty-smelling old cars. He had scored at picnics, on his mother's best couches, in homes where his dates had gone to baby-sit, but he was only eighteen years old, and no one like Ivy Hatter had ever walked into his life—and perhaps never would again.

Her efficiency apartment was upstairs over a row of antique stores off Thirty-sixth Street. No one occupied the stores, not even during the day, as if they didn't care about the businesses, so the neighborhood was mostly silent except for Ivy's practice sessions with her combo—two black guys and a stunning Danish girl who spoke little English.

"Here, over here," she told Jack that first afternoon. "Use the side of the bed. Much better here on the side and corner." Entering her body was like entering a new dimension. She was made for it. They didn't get back to sounds or synthesizers for two days.

As a lover, she was reckless, and he came to find that he was, too. They sometimes went out to lunch after sleeping together, but at night she went off into her life at the bars and clubs without inviting him. She taught him to phone before coming over to her place, and she never once wanted to visit any of his life or places. He knew that she had other men—one-nighters, always—but in the course of a week he would be with her three or four times, sleep with her perhaps two whole nights, work on her music with her for a dozen hours, and somehow this was enough. Even too much: Ivy was an intoxication. Occasionally, he had to come to the surface, sober up, and stay away from her.

"My dreams are killing me," she told him. "I wanted to be famous by this time. I'm twenty-five years old and feel like I'm slipping behind."

"You're just getting started," he argued with her. "Music's a damn tough business."

"I think about dumping the band. Then I think, no, they're my best shot. I think about adding more instruments. I think about new sounds—everything from a more traditional jazz than we play now to hard rock. Is ambition crazy?"

"I don't know," he admitted. "I haven't got much yet."

"You're a genius and don't need any," Ivy sighed. "But I dream about playing big concerts. I can't think about anything else sometimes. I'd do anything for that. I'd sell my soul, I would!"

A few times he slipped into the clubs where she and the combo played and listened to them. Ivy and the Mad Hatters—of course. He was no expert, but he knew they were special: talented, dedicated musicians who blended well together. The Danish girl's fingers flew around the guitar, the blacks were solid on drums and horn, but Ivy at the piano was a marvel: its large blackness seemed to be an extension of her emptiness,

108

and she stroked or hammered the keys by way of talking to the void.

After a couple of months, she invited Jack to make some sounds with them, but he refused, and she seemed relieved that he did.

"You can handle it," he told her. "I'd never get the beat."

For another week or two, Ivy worked with the synthesizer and sounded good but then discarded it. She missed two engagements. Depression seemed to be setting in like a change in her heart's weather.

"What's the matter?" Jack asked her.

"Hey, nothing, I'm fine," she answered. "Really, I'll be all right."

But she wasn't.

One morning, he awoke in her bed to find her sitting at her little portable keyboard in the kitchen of her apartment; she played "Funny Valentine" and wept as though her heart would break.

"You gotta see a doctor maybe," he suggested, pulling up a chair. In that sudden moment, he knew that she needed more than he could give her—professional help. "What is it? Your ambitions? Your career?"

"Oh, no, Jack," she said, weeping, "it's not that at all." But she wouldn't say anymore, and so his concern for her multiplied.

There was a great vitality in Ivy that seemed to be leaking away.

The next day, Jack went to her place in the late afternoon, hoping to see her before she went off for a night's work at a coffee house near Fairmont Park. She wasn't home, but as he left her doorstep, he ran into the black horn player, Rambo, who was looking for her, too.

"She ain't gonna show tonight," Rambo fretted. "I just know it."

"What's wrong with her?" Jack asked him.

"Hey, man, she's just drugged out."

"Drugs?"

"Not so much heavy stuff. Just lots of worrisome shit," the musician said.

"I've seen her pop a few pills and smoke a little grass," Jack admitted.

"Oh, man, she does the whole rainbow, every day since she left college. Me, I don't do that number. I like true, pure music, you know, and I can listen to the cosmos. I can be at peace, get me? I don't have to hit myself with no hammer."

"Have any idea where she is?"

"It may be time to bust up our act," Rambo said, not answering Jack's question exactly. "She does play that fine piano, man, but she ain't gonna come home to me or you anytime soon. Maybe nobody gonna find her."

That night, Jack's mother came to his bedroom and woke him up. He had gone to sleep with his earphones on, listening to an old Brubeck tape.

"Telephone," she told him, shaking him awake. "This girl is crying for you. Is this girl in trouble, Jack?"

"Coming," he said, untangling himself from the cords and blankets. He knew it was Ivy.

"Don't leave me now," she pleaded. "You got to stay with me." Her voice seemed distant and lost, and there was a deep, rumbling sound as if she spoke from some crevice opened up by an earthquake.

"Tell me where you are!" Jack yelled into the phone, calling out more loudly than necessary.

"The bowling alley," she said. "Hurry. Oh, Jack, please."

He spent his next minutes getting his shoes on and looking up bowling alleys in the yellow pages of the phone directory. He found several all-night establishments and had to guess where she might be.

He drove over to the big new lanes on Forty-sixth Street, but she wasn't there. Then he sped out Germantown Avenue. Streaks of morning light formed in the eastern sky. In the coffee shop of the next bowling alley, she sat watching the lone athlete, a disoriented drunk who bowled most of his shots into the gutter, cursed, slapped his legs in disgust, then tried again. She was in a good mood, laughing at this forlorn display.

"Watch this guy," she told Jack. "He's drunker'n a hoot owl. Watch him!"

110

"Come on," he urged her, holding her arm gently.

He led her out to his car, but by the time they got there, she seemed not to know where she was or who she was with. Her head lolled from side to side.

"What are you on?" he asked her. "Tell me, I'll help."

But Ivy was in the long, downward tunnel. "I don't know you," she told him. "You ain't even black. Don't talk to me."

This was the first of several retrievals. Jack helped Rambo and the others get her to engagements. He put her over his shoulder and carried her bodily out of Giovanni's Room, where she was the object of attention of two lesbian girls. He slept at her place during the week when she seemed to be in withdrawal from some unknown drug. He watched her neglect her food, lie, complain, and make excuses. Once, at the keyboard, she seemed to have forgotten everything, and her hands hovered in the air above the keys, her face puzzled, until she got up and went into the bathroom to cry.

Then, one day, he didn't see her anymore. He knew that he should, that no one else cared for Ivy and her problems, but he swerved out of her life and back into his own work. Ivy Hatter meant responsibility, aggravation, and doom. He went back to his sounds as if, as Rambo said, one could listen to the cosmos; in the fierce static of his consoles, he dodged the pain of weakness, love, and human frailty. In a pattern he would follow for his next years, Jack escaped into that comfortable audio dimension where he felt safe.

In the army, the same thing: it was the last days of the Vietnam conflict, and controversy raged, but he found his own electronic haven.

"The question's simple," his sergeant raged. "Will a man fight for his country or not? So it's an unpopular war! So what?"

"I suppose that's the question, all right," Jack agreed.

"Don't be sarcastic with me, Luce," his sergeant grumped at him. "There you are on your fat ass tinkering with them wires and circuits. What the hell good are you if the Commies attack us?"

"I'm working on some highly special audio theories," Jack confided, lowering his voice. "Someday —because of my research here in this little sound studio in Jersey—maybe we can beam a blast of sound at enemy rockets aimed at our cities and knock them out of the sky."

"No shit?" the sergeant asked, gaining new respect.

"Sound beams, laser rays, thermonuclear devices, those are the weapons of the future, sarge, and you better believe me," Jack said seriously, nodding his head like a sage. He put on his earphones and turned a dial. Charlie Mingus. The sergeant's face had a look of sudden new approval for this corporal. Jack, meanwhile, listened to a high jazz wail and wondered if all fighting men should be provided with tape decks and portable battery packs so they could kill the enemy while listening to their favorite rhythms.

Army life passed. Afterward, Jack went back to Philadelphia and a string of girl friends and odd jobs. He went out with Beryl, Sondra, Linda Spain (adored by his pal, Norris), and a half dozen others. His game was clearly stated: sex, companionship, no attachments, no permanency. However, of course, the fate of duty often falls hardest on those who try to escape it. When Tom Bell interviewed him about working for the Keen Commission, Jack swam out, once again, into moral waters that were over his head.

That service with the Keen Commission would finally bring him the guilt he denied he would ever have, the responsibility he cursed, the pain he had determined to live without. As an added torture, he ran into Ivy Hatter again, too.

She was back working at the Owl, tending stacks of used books and looking as frayed herself as last year's mystery novel. When she saw him come in, her lips formed his name.

"How're you doing, Ivy?" he asked in return.

"Well, I'm not playing keyboard anymore." She had a wan, soft, defeated smile that almost broke his heart.

"Bad news," he said. He wanted to touch her, but

he was afraid she might fall into his arms. "I can't believe it. Is it just temporary?"

"For a while, I thought so. But, no. I'm stopping. It's a habit I had to kick."

"You were a great keyboard player and pretty good on the synthesizer."

"I was mediocre, and I knew I couldn't ever really have my dream because that was so."

"You could've played in clubs. You could've kept on," he said, sounding more upbeat than he felt.

"You want to see how far you can go," she said, shrugging. "When you know, I suppose you can stop."

There was an awkward pause between them in which he actually read the titles off a nearby shelf.

"I'm still on drugs," she blurted out, telling him more than he wanted to either know or ask. "I just can't kick that stuff."

"Sorry, Ivy, really," he said.

"I need you, Jack," she whispered, and he knew that she needed something or someone badly but not him. Her face twisted as if she might cry. Those long fingers that had caressed the piano keys found the pale flesh inside her unbuttoned blouse and rubbed there softly, as if some inner spring had broken painfully loose.

"I'm looking for a certain book on audio tech," he managed.

"Searching for a new sound?" she whispered, repressing a sob.

"Absolutely. Still looking."

"I remember you so well," she whispered even more softly, her voice dying.

"It was wonderful back then," he told her, and she seemed to be searching his face for more. After another minute, she recovered slightly.

"Did you just come in here by accident?" she asked him.

"Yeah, really. I never guessed you'd be back here, but I'm glad you're okay."

"I'm not," she whispered.

For a long, awkward moment, they stared beyond each other.

"Well, we don't carry books like that," she finally managed. "Just literature, humanities, the general stuff —nothing technical."

"I didn't think you'd have it," he said. His body twitched in yearning for her, and for the faintest moment he could feel her old warmth and imagine her there on the corner of her bed. After one night with Ivy, he was older by a lifetime.

"See you," she whispered, choking a little.

"Yeah, see you around. Soon, I hope," he told her, and with an awkward movement, almost walking backward, he somehow got out of the book shop.

In the next weeks, he entered the labyrinth: wires and bugs, good and evil cops, the comedy of Timmy DiPrima growing pot to Mozart records and the tragedy of Freddie Corso rubbing his face with his handkerchief and eating Jack's mom's popcorn. Life closed in on Jack: he had tried commitment one more time, but it had been his undoing. Women, public service, ambition were traps that drew him out of his insulation, he knew, and he swore to avoid them.

Yet here was a morning all new.

Sally slept in her beautiful curve of sleep.

Donahue hadn't called back.

Protective of a woman, committed to a cause, up to his ass in trouble, he sat by the phone in his studio wondering if he was in his right mind.

Sally isn't another Ivy, he reminded himself. Sally was tough and traveled but had hope for herself. And the McRyan matter wasn't another bog like the work with the Keen Commission. *And I'm not the same myself,* Jack told himself. *Somehow, this time I'll stay detached. I really will.*

# 16

Dressed as a telephone repairman, Burke entered Jack's building, tipped his hat to the milkman, who was leaving, and went down to the basement.

While Jack was upstairs having his coffee, Burke found the phone box. The lines to Jack's studio were clearly marked, so the bodyguard began his work. First, he disconnected the wire that would have the effect of putting Jack's phone on a permanent busy signal—a little trick he had learned while still a kid in that first army prison. Then he attached a small cassette tape recorder to Jack's system. The result was that Jack could make outgoing calls, which would be recorded for Burke's use, and could receive no incoming messages.

It pleased Burke to be handling the young technician with technology. Simple stuff, of course, but it promised to be very effective in the next hours.

Burke went outside and stood there boldly beside the stolen truck. Across town, in another basement, its door carefully locked and bolted so that anyone would have trouble getting inside, lay a dead man, the plump, unsuspecting telephone repairman whose identity Burke had borrowed. Now the rest of the list: he would stay at his work all day in spite of his headache, and everything would be settled.

He slid into the front seat of the truck, started the motor, and headed back across town.

Government by murder, he was thinking as he drove. Most of the nations of the world were conducted by assassination. Americans were naive—even those of the so-called right wing who imagined that this sort of blood letting wasn't necessary. *At the end of this day,* he promised himself, *the McRyan matter*

115

*will finally be settled, and those insipid patriots in Florida, the oil man, Mr. Murray, Lawrence Henry, and all the rest will be taking orders from me.*

In the meantime, Sally roused herself from her sleep. She came awake with a smile to find Jack sitting by the phone, a cup of steaming coffee in his hand.

"Good morning, my love," she rasped.

"Hey, hello. Get dressed, will ya? Lots going on."

"Is that any way to greet me?" she asked, rising on one elbow so that the blanket fell away from one breast. When he didn't reply, she climbed to her feet and padded across the floor to kiss his cheek. "What's the matter?" she asked.

"I want you to take a taxi to your apartment, get into a conservative suit, pack your overnight bag, and stay ready to move," he told her. His voice was so somber and he sounded so logical that she poured herself a cup of coffee and began to dress even as he finished. "Make the taxi driver go into the apartment with you, check things out, and then lock up tight when he's gone. Wait for my call. I've got to wait here for Donahue to phone me back."

"You called him? What did he say?"

"He couldn't talk, but we'll make a deal for the film. My hunch is that he'll want me—or both of us—on his television show. And I think it's a good thing."

She zipped her skirt and began combing out her hair. "Why both of us? I don't know about getting on TV. Christ, I don't need any more exposure."

"An audience will believe two of us better than it will believe one of us alone. And I want you to do this, Sally, for your own protection. We want things in the open now. No more cover-up."

"Well, I'll think about it."

"Believe me, this is the only way. You've got to trust me."

She came over to him and rubbed the back of her hand across his cheek. "That's a familiar line," she said, smiling.

"I mean it," he said, trying to impress on her the severity of their situation. "Go home, make sure your

116

apartment is safe, lock yourself in, and wait for my phone call. Got it?"

"Yes, yes," she said, and kissed him beside his ear. "Hey, I think I love you," she added.

"Yeah, love you, too," he mumbled, pulling her close, although his thoughts were clearly miles away.

The excavation site, meanwhile, swarmed with police cars, plainclothes detectives, and the special forensic van used for examining physical evidence in murder cases. Teams of experts had been carefully going through the mud that morning since finding the corpse of the young woman; they examined the smeared walls of the excavation where the victim and her killer had slid down into the pit below, took blood samples, and looked for hairs, fibers from clothes, and other clues. A crowd of people from the neighborhood had gathered to watch, and some of them had to step aside to let a telephone company truck ease by.

Inside it, Burke smiled. He was returning to the scene of his crime, in plain view and unnoticed.

The Bond Hotel still sported its broken neon; only two letters, O N, flickered in the noontime glare. The telephone company truck pulled into the loading zone, stopped, and Burke got out. He went around to the service door of the hotel but found it locked, so he presented himself at the lobby.

"Come to check a line," he told the drunken clerk.

"Go ahead," the man said, waving an arm.

Burke spun the register around so that he could read its names.

"You need somebody?" the clerk asked, more interested than before.

"Yeah, somebody called in a complaint. Resident here."

"Wouldn't nobody here do that," the clerk said, still not rising from his chair to confront Burke's intrusion.

"Just thought it might be a resident," Burke said. "No problem." He already had the information he needed. There was no Manny Karp listed, but the only two males registered were on the second floor, and it would be no trouble finding his quarry.

Without allowing further conversation, Burke picked up his tool kit and trudged upstairs. The stairway creaked under his weight, as if it might be sounding an alarm, but the desk clerk was already unconcerned once again. This was a place of derelicts and drifters, occasional whores and down-and-out schemers, which, in the clerk's opinion, Manny Karp and all his photographic equipment fully represented.

Burke had to choose between rooms 201 and 207, so he listened first at one door and then the other. Lawrence Henry had little suspected that when he gave Burke a sketch of the McRyan matter, mentioning the photographer's name, that it would come to this maverick operation. The aide, in fact, suspected little of anything; he mistook position for power, so he had little comprehension of real politics. He liked to wear his business suits, sit in overstuffed chairs in stuffier clubs, take vacations on yachts with his enemies and friends alike, and pretend that the vote and high ideals could keep America strong. They had murdered McRyan almost by accident—half planning it, half executing their plan, bungling the cover-up, permitting such scum as this photographer to endanger them.

Burke knocked at the door.

"Yeah?" Karp called through the closed door.

"Got to check a telephone line," Burke answered.

As he opened the door, Karp griped, "Hell, can't you let a guy work. You see I'm busy and—"

He was unable to say anything more. In a single flow of movement, Burke entered, dropped the tool kit, opened the wire from his Rolex case, and found his quarry's throat. The movement was like a dance step —quickly maneuvered, silent, elegantly deadly. As Karp grabbed at Burke's thick wrists and began his struggle, his killer reached back gently with one foot and closed the hotel door behind them.

There was little sound: the scraping of Manny Karp's feet on the floor as he was twice, three, four times, lifted up. Blood oozed out of the wire as it bit into his flesh. His eyes protruded, and his tongue, busy as always, lolled against one side of his mouth and then the other.

In that moment that the door was opened, Burke

had seen the photographic equipment toward which he now slowly dragged his victim. They stood almost at the center of the room, staggering slightly. Then Karp's knees began to buckle, and he sank down, Burke kneeling with him as he dissolved; for several minutes, as the wire twisted and bit harder, they remained in this position until Burke released his quarry and allowed him to slide down quietly into death.

For a moment, Burke's own breath filled up the silence, and his head seemed to spin with pain.

The strange and awful gull, he thought, came and perched itself on the window sill. The room grew dark, then gradually light again.

After he recovered himself, he acknowledged Karp's dead body and walked over to the stack of photos beside the enlarger. There were hundreds of photos of that night—McRyan's car wreck in vivid detail for everybody to study. *The fools,* he thought. *The silly fools.* He emptied his tools on the floor, then stuffed all the photos and negatives inside his kit so that he could destroy this material later. He made sure he had everything, including each little roll and can of film.

Quietly, then, he strolled back outside to his truck.

He sat behind the wheel of his stolen truck trying to regain control. His head throbbed, yet inside him, more confused and obscure than a few hours before, there was a calendar for death. The list included that dead scum upstairs in the hotel and his cheap whore, but surely, Burke was thinking, they ought to include far more important fools than these. Surely Lawrence Henry himself. *Before the day ends,* he found himself thinking, *surely all the bunglers and fools should die.*

He caught sight of himself in the mirror outside the window of the truck. For a moment, he wanted to laugh. *I'm the most intelligent, methodical, organized person in all this,* he told himself, *and I'm crazy. I have terrible headaches, blackouts, and visions of birds, but I know what serves our cause more than any of the others.*

Burke couldn't decide who to kill next.

119

# 17

After making sure that her apartment was empty and safe, Sally locked all her doors. Judy, her roommate, wasn't there, and this worried her. Every little thing became an unsettling fear, even the click-clack of the refrigerator as it turned itself on.

She phoned Jack, but his line was busy.

As ordered, Sally gathered a few of her clothes and dressed in a modest gray suit and blouse. Old anxieties rushed her, as if she waited for a next blow; she felt as if she were on that trip West again, in that breathless pause before Stew lost his temper or before the jailer came into her cell or before she could escape from the airport in Phoenix that night.

After packing a few items in her makeup case, she phoned Jack again—the same busy signal. She felt certain that he was having a long conversation with Donahue, making arrangements, yet her fears were so strong and specific that she considered skipping out. She felt like hurrying to Reading Station again and catching that train to Miami so that Jack or anyone else would never be the wiser. She loved him as much as any man she had ever known—he had asked this important favor of her, and she wanted to grant it— but she felt the compulsion to flee, to protect herself, for once in her life, and to trust no man.

"I do love him," she told the empty room as if trying to convince herself. "And, yeah, I'll wait here. I'll stick."

She dialed his number once more—still busy.

Jack, meanwhile, sat in his studio, his phone silent, deciding whether or not to call Donahue again himself. He also strongly felt he should check on Sally but wanted to keep the phone clear for incoming calls and wait until he had news for her.

Waiting and worrying, he assembled some gear and clothes so that he and Sally could skip out soon after their job was done. He wished he had a pistol. He wished Donahue would hurry and call. Outside his window, the sounds of traffic grew loud, so he finally went over, looked out, and noted the crowded streets. It took him a moment to realize that today was the Liberty Day celebration and that all the streets, bars, hotels, and restaurants in the downtown area would be packed. He wondered if Donahue and the television people were busy with all the hoopla or if somehow, in some way, the media was actually involved in a suppression of facts concerning McRyan's death.

While Jack fretted, the Liberty Bell hawker danced and cavorted for a stream of tourists who filed into the lobby of the Hilton Hotel. Along the streets and around the historic squares and buildings, thousands of celebrants were already milling around. Unnoticed in the throng at the Hilton, then, were the number of somber men gathered in the penthouse suite.

There were drinks on a large, round, mahogany table, but none of the men were interested in refreshments or social conversation. The oil man wore his Stetson and Mr. Murray of New York tugged nervously at his raw-silk tie. Lawrence Henry and a deputy police commissioner paced the floor.

"So if we can't find Burke today, gentlemen, we're going to have to proceed as if he has carried out the mission he described to me," Henry explained.

"Old Burke is a good man," the oil man drawled. "I think we can count on him to do what he says."

"He scares me," Mr. Murray admitted. "Always did."

"We've looked for him," the deputy commissioner added. "It wouldn't be tactful if we put out an all-points bulletin, but I've arranged help searching for the man with some cops I trust."

"What about the sound technician?" Henry asked him.

"We'll stake him out if you want," the deputy said.

"Maybe we should," Henry said, trying to decide. "And the girl, too—the one in Karp's photos."

"I'll get on the phone if you say so."

"What do you think, Mr. Murray?" Henry asked.

"I think we all talk about violent means, favor them, discuss the necessity of them, but in real situations like this grow afraid. I know I do."

"But, theory aside, what should we do about Burke?" Henry asked.

"I just don't know," Mr. Murray admitted.

The phone rang, and the deputy commissioner strolled across the room to answer it. He talked in hushed tones while the others continued.

"There are one or two other possibilities," the oil man suggested, sucking on a lemon wedge that he took from a little bowl beside the liquor bottles. "We could make an all-out effort to stop Burke today. Or we could let him do his work, then kill him ourselves. Or we could actually elevate him in the organization as he suggests."

"We wouldn't want him sitting in on our council meetings," Mr. Murray offered.

"Why not?" the oil man asked. "He's effective. He delivers. He's willing to take care of the loose ends in this fucked-up McRyan matter."

"I won't be criticized," Lawrence Henry put in.

The deputy commissioner returned to the group and said, "My sources report that Karp's been murdered. I left word to be called, especially if anything showed up on Karp. There's a squad car at a little hotel right now."

For a moment, the men stood looking at each other.

"You may as well know the rest of what Burke told me," Lawrence Henry finally said. "He said that if any of us gets in his way, he'll kill us, too."

"Oh, my god," Mr. Murray said.

The oil man laughed out loud.

"I believed him," Lawrence Henry added.

"Lord, I believe him, too," the oil man said with a grin. "Burke's a real patriot and a one-man army and so efficient he makes the rest of us look sorry. I wouldn't want to cross him."

"But we do have to make a choice," Lawrence Henry said, taking charge of the meeting again with his formal tone. "And I think our friend from Little Rock has put it succinctly: we can stop him, let him do his day's work and eliminate him later, or give him the new status he wants. I favor letting him complete this round of activity. Then we'll eliminate him later."

"The city's so crowded that we really can't take the first option," the deputy said. "We won't find him today. About the rest, I have no opinion."

"I agree with Henry," Mr. Murray said.

"I vote to promote Burke," the oil man said. "But I see that my vote loses. One thing I might ask: who's gonna kill our killer later on?"

"Arrangements can always be made," Mr. Murray said, sniffing.

"They better be good arrangements," the oil man told him.

The deputy commissioner excused himself, saying he was on his way to the Bond Hotel in order to confiscate any incriminating evidence. For a few minutes after he left, the others lingered in the suite. They were similar men ideologically but very different otherwise: a Philadelphia administrator, an Ozarks millionaire, a New York dilettante. They were cordial but busy men who had to go their ways, too, so one by one they left the suite and took the elevator back down into the crowded streets outside the hotel.

The oil man drove himself in his rented Buick to the outskirts of the city where the roads began to turn down lanes overhung with bright trees. There was a colonial look to the countryside: rolling meadows adorned with cattle, gray-stone walls marking property boundaries, stately homes. At a rambling, old yellow-stucco house, the oil man parked in the curved driveway and entered. As he entered the door, a servant took his coat and Stetson and provided him with a white starched apron, which he tied on; this was the uniform of the old club, always worn by members and guests.

In a drawing room, the oil man shook hands with a congressman from Pittsburgh. As they drank their first highball, Burke arrived.

"How did it go?" Burke asked as the servant brought him a drink.

"About as we thought," the oil man told him.

When a bell rang, they filed into the low-ceilinged colonial kitchen. Guests were kitchen helpers, chopping lettuce for the salads or peeling onions, while the congressman and other regular members prepared the lunch. Burke's nerves seemed to settle in the process, and the men talked and worked beneath walls hung with bright copper pots. From the kitchen windows, one could look out on the lawn where other club members were playing shuffleboard.

They ate their simple roast lamb, vegetable, salad, and dessert in a small hall filled up with massive mahogany furniture.

"Can you do everything we've talked about today?" the congressman asked Burke at one point. The question came casually, as if the man had just commented on the asparagus.

"It should take about three hours this afternoon," Burke answered.

After lunch, they went into the great hearth in the main hall where the club's special punch was served.

"Gives the belly a very good feeling," the oil man said, and everyone agreed.

"Fine place," Burke commented. "I'd say this punch has been mulling a long time. Am I right?"

"Yes, hours," the congressman said. "You're quite a man, Burke. I'm told you appreciate fine food and know your wines."

"I know we'll have many good dinners together," Burke replied. "But now I've got to be going."

"Watch yourself," the oil man told him.

"My business is a damned cautious one. Never worry," Burke said.

The three of them shook hands and said their good-bys. Beyond, clusters of other members left them to their conversation; the voices in the room were hushed and soft and seemed, to Burke, very important. He was pleased to be in this old, traditional club, one of the seats of power. Up from prison to this world of old money, conservatism, strength—he felt proud of himself—but cautious here, too. It was a day of betrayals, and the day, he suspected, would lengthen; in the dizzying world of violence, a vertigo usually set in. Betrayal was a liquor that made men drunk more quickly than this tasty old punch.

Burke went back to his car, which was parked at the servants' entrance. He felt slightly tipsy, but there was only a trace of his headache remaining. He took deep breaths of air, got in, and drove off.

While the lunch was in progress, Jack finally became anxious enough to phone Donahue. Their conversation was recorded on Burke's little cassette recorder in the basement below Jack's studio.

"I tried calling you, but your line was busy," Donahue told him.

"Funny. You must've got the wrong number. I've been here waiting."

"Well, anyway, I'm glad you called. Of course, I want the film with your soundtrack. And I need you on the show with me, Jack, or all the film in the world doesn't mean a damn. Understand? You've got to tell my audience what you were doing there, how it happened, and then explain to them what they're seeing. You gotta make them understand the images they'll be seeing on the Karp film. Get me?"

"Yeah, I understand," Jack replied.

"And you'll do it? You'll appear personally?"

"Yes."

"Okay, what about the girl? She was there. And we'll want to talk about the cover-up. Can we get her on, too?"

"She was there, all right," Jack said, "but is there any way we can keep her out of this? She's not exactly proud of what she did."

"She has to do this," Donahue insisted. "Can I talk to her?"

"Sure, if you want to. It's up to her. I asked her to help us, but any final decision's up to her."

"Fair enough," Donahue answered. "Now, Jack, if you've got the real thing, we'll go with it on the eleven o'clock news tonight and scoop every newspaper and television network in the country by hours. Tomorrow, if we've got what you say, every reporter in the country will want another interview with you. But

I'll set up a meeting for later today so my people can view the film and judge it. Okay with you?"

"That's fine."

"Now a big question: what's the cost to us, Jack?"

"Just get it on the air. Do it right. That's all the cost there is."

"Great, Jack. I'm glad you see it that way. We'll do our best for you. And I'll get back to you later to set up the meeting."

While Burke's tape whirred away, recording all this, Jack and Donahue said their good-bys, and Jack dialed Sally's number. She picked up the phone after half a ring.

"I talked to Donahue, the TV guy," he began. "I think I trust him a little better, and we're going with this thing. I agreed to appear on his show—to explain Karp's film. He's calling me back to set up a meeting."

"I've tried calling your number for hours," Sally protested, but Jack didn't make a connection and kept talking.

"Listen, Sally, he wants you, too. The film and tape don't mean anything without our testimony and interpretation."

"Jack, I've been thinking of splitting. This isn't for me," she argued.

"Sally, this is the safest thing for us to do. People won't say that both of us are lying, and if we can get all this out in the open, nobody can hurt us."

"Yeah, I know the argument," she said. "But, oh, Jack, I don't want to have to trust anybody. I want to rely on myself."

"I honestly believe this is our best way to go," he told her.

"Okay, I'll think about it. I won't leave."

"Good, hang on until we hear from Donahue again."

Burke's first stop that afternoon was Jack's basement where, again, dressed as the telephone repairman, he removed the portable recorder.

He listened to the conversations with Donahue and Sally; then, slowing the tape speed on the casette, he returned to the place where Jack dialed Sally's phone number. Carefully, he listened and noted the number of digits clicking off during the dialing process until he knew her phone number.

It amused him, again, to think how he was using this little know-how against that meddling technician upstairs.

Burke made sure that Jack's phone was still fixed to give off a busy signal, then took his recording device and left the basement. He drove two streets over until he found a drugstore with enclosed telephone booths.

At the prescription counter, he bought aspirin, then went over to the booths, closed himself inside one of them, and phoned Sally.

Sally, waiting for Jack to call again, had grown so agitated that she poured herself a stiff drink. She sat at the kitchen table, paced the living room, tried to read a magazine, and tried to think, but her mind was numb with worry.

The jangle of the phone startled her.

"Hello?" Burke said when she didn't speak right away.

"Yes?"

"Sally Badina?"

"Who wants to know?"

"Frank Donahue—from television. Your friend Jack Luce told me to call you about the film and sound tape."

"I thought you were supposed to call him," she said.

"Damndest thing, but his phone has been busy all day. Can't reach him. So I thought I'd go ahead and phone you."

"What for?" she asked, her nerves stinging the flesh beneath her clothes. She couldn't help herself. She wanted to help, but she was overwhelmed with suspicion.

"Sally, I've got to level with you," Burke went on. "I need both of you on my show. Maybe we could meet—just the two of us. I want to convince you that this is the thing to do. Jack won't take payment, but something could be arranged separately for you."

"I don't know," she fretted.

"Tell you what," he continued, "bring that tape and film along if you have it, and we'll wrap this whole thing up. What do you say?"

"I'll have to talk to Jack about it," she said. "When and where do you want to meet?"

"I've got two very important related matters to attend to," he told her. "Should take me, oh, a couple of hours. But let me give you an address where we can rendezvous. That all right?"

She wrote down his suggestion on a pad beside her phone. Her hand trembled, she noticed, as she scribbled the information.

"This is the right thing for you to do," Burke assured her. "The best thing you'll ever do for yourself. You'll see."

# 18

Mr. Murray always traveled in his own plane, Burke knew, with a pilot named Taps who carried a 9 mm. hand gun strapped inside his blue blazer. Taps was an ex-marine who said little, knew even less, and who managed to stay close to Mr. Murray's side on all trips, looking both more efficient and more protective than he actually was. Mr. Murray had ordered Taps to stop chewing gum and had designed the blazer as a sort of uniform with a tiny insignia—part of Mr. Murray's family crest—on the pocket over Taps's heart.

When they flew to Philadelphia, as Burke had once or twice done with them, they used a little private airport on the river. The Cessna was stored in a secondary hangar across a taxi strip from the office and main flight desk.

"Hello, Taps," Burke said to the pilot that afternoon.

As usual, Taps was giving the plane a final check before calling crew members to roll it out on to the taxi strip. Mr. Murray insisted on this procedure, trusting no one else, and while Taps conducted the exercise, his boss checked the weather and flight plan back to New York.

"Burke," Taps replied, looking up from the wing where he had been checking flaps. "Didn't know you were going back with us. How you been?"

The response was so friendly and so convincingly innocent that Burke smiled.

"I've been fine," Burke answered, coming around the wing. "Same old chores?"

"Yeah, same thing. Mr. Murray ain't changed none."

When Taps looked up again, Burke put an ice pick into the man's forehead just above his nose. The wound was delivered like a blow, quick, vicious, and hard, knocking the pilot down. He would never regain consciousness.

For a second, Burke stood there watching him. His own head pulsed slightly with pain, but he steadied himself, turned, and went out the rear door toward his car. Then he drove around the parking lot and emerged at the office where Mr. Murray had to be.

His former employer was many things: heir of a wealthy Long Island family, bisexual, part-time dabbler in politics, the theater, the literary and arts scenes, much else. He wore expensive clothes and enjoyed being seen with celebrities. But all his interests were casual, as if he played at life. He had no real relationships or obsessions, no causes or convictions. And now, having dabbled at a serious business too long, having put his money into the hands of much more determined men, he was going to pay the price.

A man doesn't play at politics, not even in America where the game sometimes takes on the veneer of entertainment, Burke wanted to explain to Mr. Murray.

The little airport—just as Burke recalled—was badly operated and understaffed. The two men who comprised the lazy ground crew would be off somewhere having coffee. A dumb girl would be handling charts, ticketing, and all the business of the flight desk.

Burke opened the front door quietly, slipping into a hallway, which kept him out of view. He listened but heard no voices.

Looking into the waiting room, he saw that the girl—he remembered her, too—was alone behind her counter. Mr. Murray's pile of Gucci luggage was stacked for loading. Sizing things up, Burke concluded that his former employer could only be down in the men's room.

Smiling and walking in, Burke turned toward the men's room with a long stride. Since he seemed to know where he was going, the girl paid him little attention.

Inside the men's room, Burke stopped and looked around, noting the heavy smell of disinfectant, the drip of a faucet, and broken tiles above the lavatory. Mr. Murray was inside one of the toilet stalls, so Burke entered the other one, sat down, and waited. Then, as Mr. Murray finished and went out to the lavatory to wash his hands, Burke waited again: one beat, two, three.

At last, Burke came out.

Mr. Murray was drying his hands on a paper towel. With no mirror over the basin, he couldn't see what came toward him.

Then the wire bit into his neck.

To let him know who had him, Burke spoke. "It's me, Burke," he said, "and good-by, Mr. Murray."

The struggle suddenly grew fierce, as if terror—the sound of Burke's voice, perhaps—had pumped adrenalin into the victim's blood stream, giving him added strength. They banged against a toilet stall so heavily that Burke worried about the noise. Then Mr. Murray kicked at him heavily. The blow hurt but also caused his former employer to stumble; they staggered over to the narrow little window where sunlight brightened the tiny beads of blood on the wire.

Mr. Murray kicked again, missing, and lost his balance once more until Burke lowered his victim into a urinal.

There, with his head in that smelly bowl, Mr. Murray died.

For a minute, Burke recovered his breath. Then he combed back his hair with his fingers, straightened his tie, and walked out again, taking long strides across the waiting room once more. He got into his car and drove off. As he passed the hangar across the way, he saw those two crew men, laughing together, strolling back to work.

As he drove back from the airport, traffic increased. The crowd for the Liberty Day celebration was growing. On the car radio, a newscaster gave details of a preliminary investigation into Governor McRyan's death. *"The commission has concluded,"* the announcer said, *"that Governor McRyan died in a freak accident."* Burke was still smiling as the announcer began talking about the murder of a girl at an excavation site and warned women in the center of the city to be cautious alone on the streets.

*In two or three hours, I'll be out of here,* Burke said to himself, *and you can have the city of brotherly love to yourselves.*

By the time he had reached the center of the city, his head ached again. He swallowed more aspirin and stopped for another phone call. The oil man's information on the whereabouts of Lawrence Henry had been sketchy, but Burke called a secretary who obligingly provided two more phone numbers. After another call, the former aide was located at Governor McRyan's old office.

"Will Mr. Henry be there all afternoon?" Burke inquired.

"Would you like to ask him personally?" yet another secretary asked.

"No, I wanted to see him. Don't disturb him."

"I believe he'll be here at least another hour," the secretary said. "Who shall I say is calling?"

Burke hung up.

The office building overlooked Independence Square, so Burke could see the crowds of celebrants below when he reached the tenth floor. For a moment, he stood outside the elevator peering down into that green patch of grass and trees adorned with the famous white steeple.

In a corner of his mind, he imagined that all this history and tradition were in his brutal keeping; then, for a scant moment, he realized also—in a crazy tumble of recognition—that he didn't want to kill another man. He wanted another woman in his last embrace. He wanted the feel of her last twitchings. He wanted Sally—and then, perhaps, another and another after her. For a moment, these things mixed inside him: fantasy and brave ideals.

Someone came down the hallway where he stood. Stepping inside the nearby stairwell, he hid himself and waited.

A man and a woman waited for the elevator. From a glass panel in the stairwell door, Burke could watch them as they finally stepped inside and were gone. He decided to wait where he stood. In time, Lawrence Henry—perhaps alone—would come to that same spot and push the elevator's lighted button.

For more than half an hour, Burke stood watching the elevator, his head throbbing, his thoughts tumbling with confused dreams. He held to the door frame much as he had held, long ago, to that dead log in the swollen waters of the river; the same darkness came to him, as if night had overtaken him, and he floated in the desperation of his flight.

At last, a man stood at the elevator, alone and waiting. Although his back was turned to Burke, Lawrence Henry was easily recognized. In seconds, Burke gathered himself for his next task. *If I do this one last exercise,* he told himself, *I'll have Sally all to myself to enjoy. This one last chore.*

As the elevator door opened, Lawrence Henry stepped inside. Burke could see that his victim was alone, so with swift timing he moved out into the hallway. The doors of the elevator had almost closed when Burk pressed the down button once more, opening them again. For the first time, Lawrence Henry saw who was with him, and his lips released a small, faint, sighing sound.

Burke switched on the stop button, holding the

closed elevator in place. The rest took less than five minutes.

# 19

Jack, still waiting for the phone call that wouldn't come, watched television as the early-evening newscaster discussed the findings on McRyan's death. Police Detective Mackey was being interviewed and was just beginning to explain how accidental events were, but an urgent knock at Jack's door prompted him to switch off the set.

"Jack! It's Sally! You in there?"

Jack crossed the room, opened the door, and let her in. She seemed excited and greatly relieved to see him.

"What's the matter? You were going to wait until I called," he reminded her.

"Something's wrong with your phone. I tried to call but kept getting a busy signal," she told him.

"I haven't used the phone all afternoon," he said, crossing over and picking up his phone receiver. The dial tone sounded safe and normal. "I've been waiting for Donahue's return call."

"He's been trying to call you, too, but gets a busy signal," she said. "So he called me. He wants to meet me at the Thirtieth Street station at five o'clock."

"How'd he get your number?" Jack wanted to know.

"You didn't give it to him?"

"No."

"Well, he's a reporter. He's probably got his ways. He said that I could give him the tape and film."

"Yeah, he wants to screen the stuff," Jack said.

"And he wants to talk to me about going on his show."

"Funny, he said he would call me back."

"Maybe the phone company's in on the conspiracy. Come on; your phone's out of order. Let's give him the film and get things over with. What's the matter with you? You worried now?"

"A little, yeah. Let's see, he wants to talk with you, right?"

"Listen, Jack, on the way over here, I decided, okay, I'll do everything Jack wants me to. I'll see Donahue. I'll talk on TV. Now you're fidgeting."

"I'm not in the mood for a double-cross," Jack said. "So let's do it this way: you meet him, talk to him, and if he sounds all right, give him the film."

"And where are you gonna be?"

"Very near."

"I don't get it. You could come with me."

"I'm going to wire you. If Donahue disappears with the film or crosses us in any way, we'll have him on tape so he can't pretend he didn't take it."

"Aren't you getting paranoid? I mean, he's a newsman, and this is a big story. Why wouldn't he want to put this on the air? Why would he run off with the film?"

"What's wrong with covering ourselves?" Jack asked.

"Okay, what exactly is a wire anyhow?"

"Unbutton your dress and I'll show you," he said.

At Independence Square, Burke had joined the throng of people milling around. A brass band played "Stars and Stripes Forever" on the green. Beneath a lamppost, the Liberty Bell hawker danced for a circle of appreciative tourists. From where he stood, Burke could look up toward the office building where, by this time, Lawrence Henry's crumpled body had surely been found. A newsboy passed, waving a paper whose headline boldly announced STRANGLER STRIKES. A troop of girl scouts went by bearing an oversized American flag in their arms.

Dizzy and unsteady, Burke leaned against one of the iron hitching posts. He couldn't recall, somehow, where he had parked his car. The buildings on State House Row seemed to shimmer and go out of focus.

Slowly, he remembered that he had to see the oil man before going on toward the Thirtieth Street station and the appointment with Sally. Moving through the crowd again, he looked down a side street, then across to adjacent Washington Square, where there were hundreds of noisy people. The car, he finally recalled, was at the entrance to an alley. He crossed a street, trying to get his bearings.

"You drunk?" a traffic cop asked him, taking his arm.

"No, thanks, officer," Burke replied courteously. "Feeling a little ill. And trying to negotiate this crowd and get to my car."

"Well, take it easy, sir," the cop said, and let him go.

Burke circled half a block, found the alley, got into his car, and rested his head on the back of the seat. For a moment, he worried about the stolen telephone truck, abandoned but possibly containing a fingerprint. He had tried to be careful and had worn gloves, but everything seemed to be losing focus, and he couldn't remember who or how many he had killed; he was like a warrior sick with battle, confused and weary.

The crowd moved beside the car, a couple of pedestrians bending over to peer inside at him.

Down at the end of the alley, a group of sailors stood around laughing with a young blonde hooker. They paid no attention to Burke, who slumped in his car, his head back, watching them, and their laughter filtered back up the alleyway through the noise from the crowd on the street and the music of the brass band over in the square. While the others watched, a young sailor stepped into a doorway with the girl.

Burke watched as if a fever had come over him.

The sailors circled the doorway, obscuring a good view, but it was clear what was happening. They were down there with garbage cans, refuse, the grimy back doors of shops and stores; the hooker was on her knees servicing the sailor; others touched themselves and groaned, the sound of their young voices drifting back toward Burke. He felt himself stirring with desire and a confused, brutal longing.

He started the car and drove toward the group of sailors. Slamming on the brakes, he stopped before hitting them but caused them to jump back and curse; in the doorway, the young sailor, frightened, looked up, his pants around his knees, but the girl continued her effort.

"Get out of that damn car," one of the young sailors yelled, shaking his fist as Burke backed out of the alley. "C'mere, you bastard!" *You are a very lucky boy,* Burke thought, *that I won't get out and bother with you.* The car swerved into the street, narrowly missing two women who walked in the crowd, then lurched into gear and sped off.

Meanwhile, Jack fixed the wire on Sally, attaching a small microphone on the clasp of her bra between her breasts.

"How far away can you hear me on this?" she asked, standing patiently in his studio while he finished.

"Well, it's a wireless," he explained, "but a good one. At a quarter of a mile, I can still get a good tape of everything you say, everything Donahue says, and all the sounds around you."

"You really think this is needed?" she asked again.

"Look, we've got nothing to lose." He made sure that her slip and bra kept any part of the wire from touching her skin. His memory of Freddie Corso and that terrible night in the old days was still vivid.

"If I had any sense at all," she said, again for the fourth or fifth time, "I'd be on a train going South, reading a magazine and worrying about how I was gonna look in my bikini on the beach."

"I can answer that," he told her, admiring her body before she buttoned up. "You'd look terrific—with or without the bikini."

Sally smirked at him.

"Here's the film and tape," he told her. "Stuff them in your bag. And remember, if you like Donahue and trust how things go, let him have them."

"And if I don't trust him?"

"In that case, I'll be listening—and I'll know better, too. Don't give him the stuff. I'll come interrupt."

"I think everything's gonna be all right, don't you?" she asked, wanting reassurance one more time.

"Sure. He's gotta listen to the tape and see the film. That figures. It sounds fine to me."

"Let's try this out," she suggested, fingering the little microphone through her blouse.

Jack switched on his cassette recorder and backed up until they were separated by the room's distance. "Okay, say something," he urged her.

She bent her head toward the mike and whispered, "I love you." When she looked up, he was smiling at her.

On Locust Street, in one of the marbled trust companies, its hallways and offices set off in deep walnut and mahogany, the oil man and the Pittsburgh congressman finished their conversation while waiting for Burke to report. They occupied a deep inner office that was adorned with darkened portraits and heavy silver ashtrays. At one time, the neighborhood had been part of a mighty Philadelphia financial empire of banks, trust companies, insurance organizations, and Republican businesses, but now the area had a shabby, genteel look. The building itself sat near the house once occupied by Joseph Bonaparte, the famous French exile, and the Musical Fund Hall where Thackeray had once lectured, where Jenny Lind had sung, and where the first Republican National Convention had once been held. The oil man listened to the congressman speak of these historic moments, but his thoughts were elsewhere. Burke's missions made him anxious. However, if successful, they would ensure a new reign in the whole country and a power and prosperity for congressmen such as this one who wanted to restore the city to its old financial and political strength.

"Yes, McRyan would be surprised if he could see us," the congressman was saying. "He was after power, too, but now we've managed to vault over his body and to get what we want. Don't you think he would be surprised?"

"He certainly would be," the oil man agreed. *Especially,* he thought, *if he could see me in this room. After all his days and nights with my wife, he would certainly be surprised to see me here.*

"Well, I'm going to leave before your man Burke arrives," the congressman said. "I hope all's gone well."

"I'm sure it has," the oil man assured him. The congressman would be surprised, too, the oil man knew, if he could guess that Burke, who he imagined to be only a highly-paid killer, was going to be part of the inner circle of friends.

They went over to a private elevator whose doors opened between the room's bookcases. "Phone me tomorrow," the congressman said, and he shook hands with the oil man and departed.

As the oil man returned to the center of the room, he picked up the ringing phone from the desk. "Yes, send him in," he told the receptionist.

As Burke entered, the oil man quickly felt that something was wrong. "You look terrible," he told Burke. "Things go wrong?"

"Everything's on schedule," Burke assured him. "I'm on my way to the last appointment."

"Both our local and New York friends are taken care of?" the oil man asked, making sure.

"That's right, both of them, but this last matter I'm going to handle a little differently."

"I've arranged our next meeting in Dallas," the oil man informed him, moving over to the desk and taking an envelope out of the drawer. "I'll let you know about the date. Here's expense money and some items of information."

"Fine," Burke said, rubbing his temples.

"You look sick," the oil man said. "Take care of yourself. How do you want to handle this last chore?"

"I just thought I might have some fun with my work," Burke answered. "By the way, did everything go all right with our congressman?"

"Perfect," the oil man drawled. "In six weeks, we'll have a completely new operation, lots of money, new leadership. With the McRyan cover-up, nobody

138

will ever be the wiser. Don't let there be any slip-ups in this last matter."

"There won't be," Burke promised.

The oil man felt a small shudder in his bones but tried to smile. He both feared and admired Burke, but at this curious moment something in the eyes and manner made him recall his wife's old complaint that the man terrified her.

## 20

Sally took a deep breath and prepared to get out of Jack's car at the Thirtieth Street station.

"If you need any help, just yell," Jack reminded her, tapping the little microphone between her breasts. "I'll come running."

"Affirmative," she said, lowering her chin toward the mike. She opened the door, got out, closed it again, tried not very convincingly to look brave, and walked a few paces away. "Over and out," she added.

The station was overcrowded with rush-hour patrons—the stairways full, the newspaper kiosks surrounded, the turnstiles clacking. Sally shouldered her way through a cluster of school kids, bumped against a fat businessman, and made her way toward the information desk. The clock over the desk made it exactly five-fifteen as she turned to look around.

"He's late," she whispered, and Jack, sitting in his car outside the station, adjusting his receiver, heard her voice clearly.

From the sixth-floor catwalk high up in the upper reaches of the station's ceiling, though, Burke watched her. She was like a speck below, moving among other specks, then stopping at the information desk. Satisfied that she was alone, he finally moved along the catwalk toward the ladder that would lead him down. His head pulsed with such a dull ache again that he wondered if his act would hold; he wanted her, but he wasn't sure that he could manage to smile and lure her away so that he could complete his plan.

As she waited, Sally nervously touched the yellow scarf she had promised to wear. Her fingers fluttered to it absently, as if by touching it she could hurry matters along.

"Sally?" Burke said, coming up behind her.

"Yes?" She turned and tried to keep her face under control. He wasn't at all what she expected. The man's neck, shoulders, and arms bulged with muscle, and he had a strange pain in his eyes.

"I'm Frank Donahue."

"Nice meeting you," she said, offering a forced smile.

"Look," he said. "I think we've got a little problem here."

"What?"

"Sounds funny, but I think I'm being followed."

"Really?" Her voice broke slightly in spite of her best resolve.

"Yeah, but I believe I know how to lose him. Come on, follow me." He led her toward the subway entrance. The crowd was still frenzied, so she accepted the hand he offered. His fingers felt like leather knots.

As their footfall echoed on the tile floor of the station, Jack gathered his gear quickly and jumped out of the car. He was running as he adjusted the earphones on his head, looking as he sped along.

"Don't go with him," he said aloud. "Don't, Sally." It was not Donahue's voice, he knew, but by the time he had reached the information desk, they were well out of sight. Then he heard the sound of a subway train: the terminal. He hugged the little cassette receiver to his waist as he sprinted toward the main waiting room.

"Where's Jack right now?" Burke asked her.

"At home—ah, resting."

"He needs rest. This has been a lot of pressure for him."

"What train are we taking?" she asked, trying to

pass along information to Jack as she stood there waiting. The place had the old smells: grease, vomit, grime, cigarette smoke, and there were also the loud, screeching subway noises.

"Don't know yet," he answered her. "We'll get out of here and then transfer. If somebody's following us, we'll throw them off. Don't worry, Sally. Did you get the tape and film?"

"Right here in my bag," she said.

Arriving in the huge waiting room, Jack looked everywhere, spinning in a circle, trying to spot them. Then his earphones gave him a clue: he heard a turnstile's unmistakeable rattle. Turning, he ran toward the large subway entrance sign. A vendor stepped in his way, then dodged, and they barely missed each other as Jack raced by.

Burke and Sally stood down at the far end of the platform, the dark subway tunnel beside them like an open mouth. Along the walls were Liberty Day posters, already covered with graffiti that a black subway worker tried to wash away with a stream of water from a hose.

Jack vaulted the turnstiles, lucky that no subway guards saw him, and hurried into the underground passage. A bewildering group of signs pointed in different directions to various trains, and he stood there, turning and looking at all of them, not knowing which way to go. Then he heard Sally's voice being helpful again.

"Franklin Bridge," she said. "Isn't that where they're having all the fireworks tonight?"

"Yeah, right, and this is our train," Burke answered. They were waiting for the train to come to a stop.

"We're going there?" she persisted.

"I parked my car there," Burke revealed. "Here, let me help you."

The earphones picked up the sounds of the interior of the subway train as they got on: voices, the rattle of newspapers, and shuffling feet.

"We're driving somewhere?" Sally asked.

"Sure, out to the TV station. It's not in town."

"Oh, I didn't know."

"It's on City Line Avenue."

"Oh," she managed, not sounding very convinced, "City Line."

Jack could hear the sounds of the subway train as it pulled away. By this time he raced down the subway steps two and three at a time. He ran toward the train waving his arms at Sally, but she didn't see him, and the doors to the train were closed and moving. To everyone else, Jack looked like just another disappointed commuter who had missed his ride.

Without waiting longer, though, he turned and sprinted back up the stairway. He passed through the exit, dashed across the waiting room once more, and hurried outside to his car. With his earphones in place, he resembled one of the spaced-out joggers who listened to rock music while running around Fairmont Park.

In his car again, he drove downtown toward City Hall Circle. In the meantime, his earphones informed him that Sally and her stranger were still on the subway train as it jostled them toward downtown, too. Sally still tried to be helpful.

"Let's see," she said, "I guess we're getting down toward Market Street."

Burke only grunted in reply.

The ring of traffic around City Hall was hopelessly congested, so Jack hit his car horn and barged right into it. Crowds lined the sidewalks. Store windows around him featured flags and wax displays of Nathan Hale, Ben Franklin, and all the others.

Instead of following the traffic around the circle, Jack cut diagonally across in front of city hall, but as his car emerged on the Juniper Street side, he ran into the massive Liberty Day parade. Surprised, he slammed on the brakes. A large float, bedecked with papier-mâché and hundreds of glowing light bulbs, moved into his path as he swerved in another direction. Missing it, Jack suddenly lost control of his car, and in seconds he had bounced on to a sidewalk, narrowly missing a cluster of pedestrians, and smashed into the plate-glass window of a store front.

His head hit the dashboard and windshield heavily, the blows knocking his earphones off. He was thinking of Sally as he rolled over and closed his eyes, not able to fight the unconsciousness that settled around him like a dull sleep.

As this happened, Sally and Burke left the subway at the end of the line, went out the exit, and walked toward Burke's car. Her uneasiness was apparent now, she felt, and she didn't know how to hide it.

"Sixteen or thirty-five?" he asked her.

"What do you mean?"

"They've only got sixteen-millimeter equipment out at the station. What's the film?"

"Oh, yeah, I think it's sixteen," she told him.

"Why don't you let me take a look just to make sure?"

"Sure, here," she said, opening her purse and taking out the film and tape.

"Hmm, okay," he said, opening the film can and checking the gauge. "It's sixteen, all right. But is this the original?"

They were at his car by this time, and he opened the trunk and dropped the film and tape inside. She wanted to run but couldn't. His voice, his size, the look in his eyes: nothing added up. He definitely wasn't a TV reporter.

"The original?" she asked. "No, Jack's got the original."

"That's no good," he said. "I have to use the original. How many copies does Jack have?"

"Just this and the original," she said, wishing immediately that she hadn't. She wished, suddenly, that she had told him there were hundreds of copies—copies in libraries, police stations, drugstores, and everyplace. "This is the same thing," she said, her argument terribly weak. "What do you need the original for? Won't this do?"

Burke's face changed as if a shadow came over it. "Where's the other film and tape?" he asked Sally. "At Jack's apartment?"

She couldn't answer because her mouth had suddenly gone dry.

He lifted his empty Rolex so that she could see it. Then, as she watched, he pulled out the sharp wire from its entrails, the wire scraping hideously on the metal casing as it emerged.

"Tell me where the other film and tape are," he commanded her, and he leveled a gaze at her. They stood in the dirty parking lot, loose wrappers blowing around their ankles; no one was close enough to call for help, and she knew exactly, somehow, what that wire was for. "Is the stuff at Jack's?" he asked, repeating the question, she knew, for the last time.

"Yes, at Jack's," she managed.

Reaching into the car's trunk, Burke pulled out a thick roll of tape. When he grabbed her and bound her mouth, she felt as if her bones had melted, as if she were all rag and emptiness, as if he could do anything he wanted with her now and it would all be worse than anything she had ever known—worse than her infamous trip West with all its indignities.

While she sat on the edge of the car's open trunk, Burke tied her arms and legs with the tape, too, and once, ever so slightly, she lifted a foot to help in the chore. She knew with certainty that he would kill her on the spot otherwise.

"I'm saving you," he told her. "I got something special for you. I've never done anything like I'm going to do with you, but that comes later."

She made a single low sound.

"Get in there," he told her, and he slammed the trunk shut on her.

Jack heard the noise of the wire grating as he emerged from unconsciousness; he remembered the sound, yet didn't, and in his daze he questioned himself, slipped back into painful sleep, and then awoke once more. Night had come, and he was in an ambulance, moving through the city streets, lights and disconnected sounds bombarding him. The earphones were draped around his neck, so with his first movement he reached down, fixed them around his head again, and listened to the last words Burke spoke to Sally.

He heard the Liberty Bell hawker, laughter, and the sound of kids. From his earphones, he heard this definite, familiar activity and knew, somehow, that Sally and the stranger had moved back to his studio apartment. How much time had passed since he had heard the wire? Was this a dream? He pushed himself up on one elbow and looked around.

An ambulance attendant sat next to the driver, paying Jack no attention. On the street, a group of paraders had wandered out in front of the ambulance, slowing and stopping it, and the driver yelled out the window and gave the celebrants a blast of the siren. "Hey, out! Outta the way!" he called, but they were drunk and wouldn't move from the street.

While this went on, Jack eased himself off the stretcher, staggered to the rear doors, opened them, and fled.

"You!" the ambulance attendant yelled after him. "Stop!" But he was gone, weaving his way through another cluster of Liberty Day well-wishers on the sidewalk and disappearing. He had no time for explanations.

From his earphones came the same confirming sound: the crazy Liberty Bell hawker, dancing and waving his flag as usual, while the kids of Jack's neighborhood raised their laughter. Running again, Jack saw a cab stand ahead—empty of taxis—and his thoughts raced about how he could get home.

Meanwhile, Burke came out of Jack's apartment with the original tape and film. The Liberty Bell hawker danced close beside him to the delight of the kids in the block.

"Get lost," Burke said.

"Well, well, well!" the hawker laughed at him, crouching low like an Indian and springing around in a circle.

Annoyed, Burke grabbed the tail of the man's coat and swung him away. The movement was so swift and violent that the hawker sprawled on the sidewalk, skinning his knee, and the kids complained loudly.

But Burke was at his car and gone.

He drove to an empty park close to the river, got out, and opened the trunk. For a moment, he looked down at Sally, who could only respond with fearful eyes and a pleading shake of her head. Then he tossed the tapes and film in beside her and slammed the trunk closed once again.

Jack heard all this, too, as he arrived at his apartment in a taxi. Around his neighborhood, the kids still yelled and laughed at the Liberty Bell hawker; their noises could be heard now both inside Jack's earphones and out. He knew he had just missed Sally and her tormentor. For a moment, he thought he detected a river noise: the deep, bellowing call of a barge horn. But he couldn't determine where or how he heard it.

Defeated, he paid off his taxi and let it go. The city was too big. If this was what he feared, and Sally was with her killer, he couldn't stop it. The street was suddenly deserted and silent, empty of kids, as he trudged up the steps to his apartment. Inside, the place was a shambles—ceiling tiles thrown everywhere. The original material was gone from its hiding place, and everything seemed lost.

Burke drove from the little park along the river front to the parking area at the boat basin. There he opened the trunk of the car again, took out the two tapes and films, bound them with more tape, weighted them with a window sash, and walked to the edge of the water. In the shadows near the car, he tossed the heavy bundle into the Delaware River.

They had parked near the Port of History Building at the basin where the main celebration of the Liberty Day festival was being held; not far off, around the building, a huge crowd gathered to see the fireworks display, to listen to the bands, and to see the replica of the Liberty Bell that had been manufactured out of the shiny pennies of thousands of school children.

As he removed Sally from the trunk of the car and began to untie her, Burke's gaze went to the upper balcony of the Port of History Building.

"Want to see a nice fireworks display?" he asked Sally as he pulled the tape from her mouth.

"Don't hurt me, please," she managed.

Jack had on his earphones again, listening.

"Keep quiet," Burke ordered, slapping her, and Jack heard the blow. Then he heard a popping noise, too, which he couldn't understand, and for an instant he worried that the wire might be burning Sally as once, long ago, Freddie Corso had been burned. The whole sickening memory came back to him in a flash as if he were living through the nightmare again, but at that moment a flash at his window corresponded with another loud pop. He rushed to the window and peered out across the river-front skyline. Fireworks. That's what it is, he suddenly knew: Sally's at the fireworks display.

The sky was illumined in reds and yellows, but Jack was thumping back down into the street, running toward the Port of History Building where the crowd cheered. He ran as if all his life—Freddie, the broken dreams of his years with the Keen Commission, his loss of Ivy, everything—depended on his rescuing Sally.

At the celebration, Burke pushed Sally into a narrow passage behind some bleachers. At a hole in a wire fence, they turned up a staircase leading to a balcony. All around them the crowd applauded the proceedings, ignoring them.

Jack could hear the crowd noise and every word spoken by an announcer who extolled the replica of the Liberty Bell.

As Jack raced along a darkened walkway that led to the boat basin, the band struck up a fanfare.

As the horns of the band blared out in a single loud note, Burke led Sally across the upper reaches of the building, unseen. Below was the crowd, majorettes, flags, and all the paraphernalia of patriotism, everyone cheering and applauding, fireworks going off. Burke and Sally were very near the replica itself, which hung in place between the two tiers of balconies at the building. As they passed near the replica, it chimed—a clear, deep, penetrating note—and Jack, who hurried around the edges of the crowd, looked directly at it. He saw them: Sally and the big man, up high, up there in the shadows above the festivities.

"Sally!" he called out, but she couldn't hear him.

The giant replica of the bell tolled again.

"Come on, up here," Burke told Sally, dragging her up another flight of stairs.

Cutting through the crowd, Jack finally reached the lower stairway and began sprinting up them. As the bell tolled again, a spray of fire illumined the sky, and the crowd groaned its approval.

By this time, Burke had pulled Sally into the dark shadows of the upper balcony. The wire was around her neck as he pulled her quivering body against his, his face against her throat, his arm encircling her breasts and pressing her tightly.

"I want to feel everything your body's about to do," he told her hoarsely.

"Oh, please," she managed. The wire was not yet choking her, just pulling her against him, and she felt that if she stirred or protested too much, he would yank it and kill her instantly.

"Get your pants off," he commanded her. "Do what I say."

"Oh, Jack," she managed.

As the bell sounded its next deep note, Jack heard his name in the earphones. He paused only a moment, then raced up the next flight of stairs, taking two and three steps at a time. Sally was screaming.

Although Burke was living out his wildest fantasy, the dark gull fluttered at his shoulder as if its wings beat lightly against him to annoy and scold him. Sally's warm, soapy smell filled his nostrils, but his head throbbed, and the next loud toll of the bell pierced him with pain. He wanted all this—the wild proximity to the crowd so that his victim would be tortured, at the end, by the almost reassuring presence of others; the warm, naked body of the girl, her flanks open to his touch; danger and death; music and blaring sound.

"Please," she begged as he touched her.

The wire snapped back into his watch case, but she couldn't think of freeing herself; his arms were a vise, groping and holding her. Then she saw the ice pick.

"No," she pleaded with him.

As the bell tolled again, Jack made it to the upper balcony. Sally saw him over Burke's massive form.

"Now I'm gonna put this up you," Burke said, moving the ice pick against her lower body. But Jack was there in a leap. He hit Burke with a shoulder, flying into him like a football blocker and knocking him off Sally.

With the bell's last toll, the band and fireworks started up again. Burke, sprawled on the floor, recovered his breath for a moment, then smiled.

"Get out of here," Jack told Sally, but she didn't move. He gave her a glance, trying to keep Burke's rising form in view. "Sally!" he repeated, but she lay there in the shadow of the balcony, soft and still, until Jack was forced to face his attacker again.

Burke pinned him against the wall in a single, quick, brutal movement, but the big man's hand, gripping at Jack's throat, found only the earphones, so that in the awkward struggle that followed, Burke couldn't choke his victim. At the same time, Jack held off the ice pick that Burke pressed closer to his face. The big man's grip and strength were overpowering, and Jack knew that he couldn't hold off much longer; the ice pick would soon be pressed into his eye.

In his last strength, Jack pushed away, turning quickly just as the ice pick slammed into the wall behind his head.

He stood at the head of the stairway, waiting. *If he rushes me now,* Jack thought, *I'll step aside so he'll fall downstairs.* It was a vain, futile idea. Too quick again, Burke leaped at him and grabbed him. The ice pick moved, piercing Jack's upper arm once, then twice, as Burke tried to move the thrusts over toward his victim's heart.

Jack heard himself cry out.

There was little time left.

As Burke made another move, shifting his weight, Jack grabbed him and threw both of them headlong down the flight of stairs.

At the bottom, Jack pushed Burke off him. Dazed, he tried to rise to his feet, but the big man lay across his legs, barely stirring, pinning him down. A warm pool of blood formed on Jack's arm—and another on the back of his head, which had caught a sharp edge in the fall.

Burke moved and struggled to his feet.

This is it, Jack felt. He's going to kill me now.

But Burke only staggered over to the rail of the balcony where he became a silhouette against a background of the fireworks display as silver streams of bright smoke decorated the night sky. The band played wildly. The bell sounded its last deep toll.

The ice pick protruded from Burke's chest, but he seemed to pay it no attention. Instead, he looked out over the crowd, his eyes glazed, his fatal gull fluttering its wings against his mind's last thoughts.

Jack looked back up the staircase, remembering Sally. Slowly, he got to his feet and went up into the darkness.

# 21

In those crowded offices and hallways above the old movie house, Sam, the producer, was striding through the rooms, a Big Mac burger in his clutch, shouting orders at his staff. Debby, the receptionist, filed her nails and read *Mad Magazine* as if her boss were a thousand miles away. Rick, his arms filled with tapes and reels, followed Sam out of one office and into another, and as Jack came in the front door, he seemed to have entered a poorly staged comedy.

"Sam wants to see you right away," Debby said, lifting her eyes for only a scant second.

"He always does," Jack said, and he edged along the narrow corridor between file cabinets and stacks of cardboard boxes.

"Well, whatcha got? Ya got it?" Sam wanted to know. A curling wedge of onion protruded from one corner of his mouth.

"Here, Rick, put this on," Jack said, handing the editor a reel of film.

"This better be good," Sam warned. "We ain't got no more time. We got a string of drive-ins waitin' for this baby!"

"You'll like it," Jack promised.

In the screening room, Jack stood against the rear

wall while Sam, filling the room with the scent of mustard and onion, plopped down in his usual theater seat. Rick ran the projector, and in the momentary darkness Jack closed his eyes and tried to think of nothing at all.

In the shower room of the college dorm, the innocent girl once again soaped herself as the intruder moved up behind her with his knife. She turned slowly to face him, her eyes wet and closed, hot water cascading down her face. As he raised the knife above her naked breasts, she opened her eyes. The sound of his asthmatic breathing reached a crescendo as he jerked the knife into her flesh.

Her scream, highly amplified by the tiles around her, was deafening and horrible. It was Sally's scream, taken from Jack's recorder, as Burke had attacked her.

Sam jumped up and dropped his hamburger. He grinned, waved at Jack, patted Rick on the shoulder, and shouted, "That's it! That's what I call a *scream!*"

He was still laughing and shouting orders when Jack walked out, passing the receptionist's desk and trudging downstairs where the noise of the traffic washed his thoughts clean.

Jack drove to his apartment where all the litter of his work greeted him: wires, tape, broken ceiling tiles, shattered glass. In order to fill up the silence, he turned on the television set as he began to pick up items that had been scattered around.

"*So last night,*" the television newscaster was saying, "*in a bloody struggle on the top balcony of the Port of History Building, the killer who has been stalking the city was himself killed as he struggled with the young woman whom he had attacked. As the huge Liberty Day crowd watched a fireworks display, the killer—whose identity is still unknown at this time—was done in with his own ice pick. So ends one of the most baffling and intriguing series of murders in Philadelphia history.*"

Jack listened in a listless, numbed stupor. His work, he somehow felt, was finished. The evidence on

151

Manny Karp's film and his own tape was lost. Sally was gone. The strange killer was dead, so he could tell no stories and could ultimately tie no loose ends in what remained a curious, almost dreamlike maze.

At the window, Jack stood with a handful of shiny, broken cassette tape and listened to the sounds of his city: the barge horns from the river, the hum of distant traffic, the echo of the wind off the gray walls of buildings.

Sally's bus, meanwhile, rounded a wide bend on Interstate 95 going south. She gazed out of the window at fields, indolent cows, ramshackle barns, and the endless string of telephone poles.

"Hi, there," the man seated next to her said. "You goin' all the way to Florida?"

"Leave me alone," she told him as she turned back to the window.

Although she wanted no part of any man right now, she could have said, Yes, I'm going all the way; I'm going down the interstate to Miami, then beyond, until I hit that causeway heading toward Key West; I'm going as far as this bus can take me and possibly even farther into that pure, black space beyond; I used to be heading West, she could have told him, but now I'm going South; there are many ways to go; there are great distances to cover and many roads that go on and on until they fall off the edge of the continent.

# RELAX!
## SIT DOWN
### and Catch Up On Your Reading!